"I'm tougher than you think. Really I am."

Brady couldn't stop his hands from wrapping around her slender shoulders and turning her toward him. There was something sweetly endearing about her that pulled at everything inside him. Something about the trusting look in her gray eyes that made him want to be her protector, her hero, her everything.

"Tough is not the way I'd describe you, Lass," he said quietly. The holes in the crocheted shawl exposed patches of skin to his hands. The soft feel of it excited him, almost as much as gazing at the moist curves of her lips. "Strong. But not tough."

Dear Reader,

Like the pages of a book, our minds are layered with memories, and as the years pass we're able to look back, read those pages and revisit the moments that make up our lives. Memories tell us the type of person we've been, point out our accomplishments and failures, and invariably guide the plans we map out for our future.

However, in *The Deputy's Lost and Found,* the pages of my heroine's memory are frighteningly blank. She has nothing to guide her, except the feelings in her heart. Can she trust them? And even more important, can she trust the sexy deputy who's vowed to keep her safe?

To find the answers, come with me and saddle up for another trip to Lincoln County, New Mexico, where the desert meets the mountains, old friends welcome new ones, and the youngest Donovan brother helps my heroine find her true home!

Thank you all, dear readers, and may God bless each trail you ride.

Stella

THE DEPUTY'S LOST AND FOUND

STELLA BAGWELL

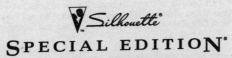

SPECIAL EDITION®

Published by Silhouette Books

America's Publisher of Contemporary Romance

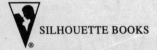 SILHOUETTE BOOKS

ISBN-13: 978-0-373-65521-2

Recycling programs
for this product may
not exist in your area.

THE DEPUTY'S LOST AND FOUND

Printed in U.S.A.

Titles by Stella Bagwell

STELLA BAGWELL

has written more than seventy novels for Silhouette Books. She credits her loyal readers and hopes her stories have brightened their lives in some small way.

A cowgirl through and through, she loves to watch old Westerns, and has recently learned how to rope a steer. Her days begin and end helping her husband care for a beloved herd of horses on their little ranch located on the south Texas coast. When she's not ropin' and ridin', you'll find her at her desk, creating her next tale of love.

The couple have a son, who is a high school math teacher and athletic coach.

To my dearest sister, Thelma Louise.

The memories we've made together
will always be etched in my heart.

Chapter One

"The woman is turning into a pest, Hank," Deputy Brady Donovan said as he steered the official SUV around a mountain curve. "Last week I told her flat out that I didn't want to go out with her again, but she's still jamming my cell phone with text messages."

The junior deputy sitting in the passenger seat offered his best explanation. "Maybe Suzie has a hearing problem?"

"Only when it comes to the word *no*," Brady muttered.

Groaning, Brady's young partner rolled his eyes toward the ceiling. "Man, if I could just be you for one day I'd overdose on women."

Brady chuckled wryly. "Trust me, Hank, a daily diet of females can be hazardous to your health."

"So is starving. And I don't want a diet of women. I want a feast. Like you."

Brady tossed his partner a droll look. "I don't know where

you get your ideas, Hank. If you ever expect to be a good deputy you've got to do a better job at sizing up people."

"Yeah. Just like you could size up Suzie's figure?"

Chuckling again, Brady rolled his head to ease the stiffness that had been building in his shoulders for the past hour. "You sound just like my family. They have this notion that I'm a cowboy James Bond. Thrilling chases after criminals and making love to a bevy of beauties. They don't understand that we spend hours on the road, talking about nothing, and wishing an antelope would cross the road just to break the monotony."

Moving to the edge of his seat, Hank twisted the rearview mirror so he could study his freckles. "Cowboy James Bond. I wish. Maybe it would change my luck if I ordered my iced tea shaken and not stirred?"

"Damn it all, Hank, straighten that mirror before it snaps off. Or do you want to explain to Sheriff Hamilton why our vehicle needs repairs?"

It was nearing ten-thirty on a pitch-black Sunday night in August. For the past two hours Brady and Hank had been patrolling the southeastern corner of Lincoln County. Not a simple feat, considering the New Mexican county covered more than four thousand, eight hundred square miles and some of the roads were rough dirt, winding through steep mountains. But Brady and his partner both knew that if criminals were out to smuggle drugs, do illegal deals or rustle some rancher's livestock, it would most likely occur on these secluded back roads. And there was nothing that Brady liked more than catching a criminal in the act. Liked it much more, in fact, than cozying up to Suzie Pippin on a cold night, or even a hot one, he thought wryly.

But so far this evening, everything appeared to be quiet. Another quarter mile to go and they'd be at Highway 380 near Picacho. Brady would be glad to get back on asphalt. Deep winter snows, followed by unusually heavy spring rains, had washed out huge sections of this particular road. He'd spent the past thirty minutes wrenching the steering wheel one way and the other in order to dodge deep holes and road ledges that were crumbling away to the steep canyons below.

"Aw, Brady, you're no fun tonight. You could've let me dream for another minute or two." Hank readjusted the mirror to its proper position and settled back in the bucket seat.

"You can dream while you're in bed," Brady retorted.

Hank sighed as he stared out at the empty dirt road in front of them. "Okay, I'll put the dreaming on hold. When we get to 70 let's head into Ruidoso. The Blue Mesa stays open all night and I want some coffee and maybe a piece of cherry cream pie," Hank said as the SUV bounced over another rough spot. "No. Make that apple. With cinnamon on it. And some ice cream on top of that."

"Forget it. We're driving on to the county line. Sheriff Hamilton didn't send us over here to eat pie. Or dream about women. Which is all you seemed to be doing tonight."

"Hell, what else is there to do?" Hank countered. "This night is as dead as a doornail."

Brady slowed the vehicle as they crossed a washboard surface in a road that had narrowed down to little more than a dirt track hugging the side of the mountain.

"Okay," he relented. "After we reach the county line, we'll head back to Ruidoso and—" All of a sudden, Brady stomped on the brakes and the vehicle skidded to a stop in the middle of the road. "Hellfire! What's that, Hank?"

Sensing the urgency in Brady's question, the other man bolted upright in his seat and leaned toward the windshield. "Where? I don't see—"

Before he could finish, Brady rammed the gearshift in Park and jumped to the ground. Grabbing a flashlight, Hank quickly followed and lengthened his stride to catch up with his partner.

"Over there," Brady instructed. "To our left. In the ditch. It looked like a body to me."

The orb of the flashlight swung to a steep cliff covered with boulders, scrubby pinyon pine, juniper and tall clumps of sagebrush, then dropped to a white object lying in the ditch.

"Man, oh, man, somebody met up with some trouble!" Hank exclaimed in a hushed tone.

"Yeah."

Before moving to the downed figure, Brady took a few seconds to assess the situation. There were no other vehicles to be seen or any evidence of a driving mishap. No persons or animals. Nor a sound to be heard. Like Hank had said earlier, the night was dead. Brady only hoped to God that wasn't the case for the person lying several feet away.

"Call this in, Hank."

To the onlooker, the two deputies appeared equal and for the most part they shared duties just as they shared a friendship. But during critical calls, Brady's position of chief deputy demanded that he take control. Thankfully Hank was more than happy to accept the protocol.

"Right," Hank replied. "An ambulance, too?"

"Let me have a look first. We might need the coroner."

The other man tossed Brady the flashlight, then made a quick U-turn back to their unit. Brady moved purposely forward, his gaze surveying the body lying facedown on the rocky ground. The person was slender, dark-haired, dressed in blue jeans and white shirt and unfortunately showing no sign of life.

Homicides were extremely rare in the county. In fact,

during his seven years at the sheriff's department, Brady had only worked two murder scenes. The last thing he wanted was a third.

His senses on keen alert, he squatted near the body and, using one hand, swiftly slid his finger to the artery at the side of the victim's neck, the flashlight throwing a narrow beam of light. The faint pulse fluttering against the pad of Brady's finger sent relief rushing through him.

Behind him, the sound of crunching gravel alerted him to Hank's approach.

"Is he alive?" the other man asked quickly.

"Yes. But unconscious."

Very carefully Brady rolled the person to a face-up position and was instantly whammed with shock as he found himself staring at a young woman! One side of her black hair was wet with blood, while dried smears marked her forehead.

"Hank, get a blanket from the unit and call for an ambulance," Brady ordered swiftly. "It's a woman. And she has a nasty gash on the forehead."

While the other deputy hurried away, Brady carefully searched her limbs for obvious broken bones or visible injuries. Other than the head wound, there didn't appear to be any, but he could only guess what might be going on internally. Except for a crumpled tissue, there wasn't anything in her pockets.

Hank arrived with the blanket and as Brady folded it to make a cushion for her head, the woman suddenly made a faint groaning noise.

Encouraged by the sound, Brady stuffed the makeshift pillow beneath her head, then questioned, "Miss? Can you hear me? Wake up and tell us what happened! Is there anyone else injured?"

She groaned again and Brady glanced at Hank. "What's the ETA on the ambulance?"

"Twenty-five minutes. When it's time, I'll drive to the highway to signal them," Hank told him. "Unless you'd rather me stay with her and you do it."

Brady wasn't about to leave the woman. Everything about the situation was screaming that some sort of foul play had taken place and he wanted to be around to make sure nothing else happened. "I'm staying," he said bluntly.

"What the hell could she have been doing way out here?" Hank wondered aloud.

"I can't make sense of it," Brady responded. "She doesn't look like the typical person involved in drug use or trafficking. And this area isn't a national forest with camp sites or hiking trails for nature lovers. I don't want to start speculating, but I'm getting a bad vibe."

"Could be she had a simple accident," Hank suggested.

"Yeah. But why did a simple accident happen in the middle of nowhere?"

"Maybe she's been out hunting. Her vehicle might be parked on one of the offshoot roads and we didn't spot it."

"Maybe. But there's no rifle or bow and hunting season is closed. Besides, she isn't dressed for that sort of thing. Look at those cowboy boots. Small fortune for those hand-stitched babies. And she's wearing turquoise—the expensive kind—on her wrist and neck. A robber wouldn't have left that behind."

"Hmm. That's why you're the chief deputy," Hank said wryly. "You don't have to study about noticing things. You just see them."

Brady glanced up at Hank. "Walk the edge of the road and see if you can spot a wallet or handbag lying around," he ordered, then, turning his attention back to the victim, he lifted her hand and patted the back of it. "Come on, miss, wake up!"

This time his voice must have penetrated. Her eyelids fluttered, then slowly lifted. Brady anxiously watched her gaze attempt to focus on him.

"Hello," he said to her. "Welcome back."

She stared blankly at him. "What—where…am I?"

Even though her voice was dazed and weak, Brady was relieved to hear her speak. Bending near, so that she could get a look at his face and official uniform, he explained, "I'm Chief Deputy Brady Donovan."

"A deputy?" she repeated dazedly. "Have I…been in some sort of accident?"

"It appears that way." He squeezed her hand. "An ambulance is on the way. Other than your head, does it feel like anything else is injured?"

Her free hand slowly lifted to her temple. "My…head is…pounding."

"Anything else hurt?"

She closed her eyes and for a moment Brady feared she was going to lose consciousness again.

"No— I…don't think so," she mumbled.

Encouraged that she might not be as badly injured as he'd first feared, he asked, "Can you tell me anything? What happened?"

Confusion puckered her forehead. "No. I— Where am I?"

Brady pulled a handkerchief from his pants and began to wipe at the blood trickling near her eye. If someone had deliberately struck this lovely young woman, they'd obviously left her for dead. The idea sent a shudder down his spine. "You're on a mountain road in Lincoln County, New Mexico. You don't remember?"

Her eyes widened and Brady could see they were a deep gray, the color of a snow cloud on a stark winter day. They were framed by black winged brows and long thick lashes that fluttered like a silk curtain caught in the wind.

"New…Mexico? I—" She broke off as her trembling fingers traveled from her forehead down to her dirt smeared cheek. "That doesn't…make sense to me."

"Why?"

"I…don't know! It—" Suddenly in a panic, she attempted to rise. Not wanting her to struggle and perhaps worsen her condition, Brady helped her to a sitting position. By now, her whole body was beginning to shake, a signal to him that she might be slipping into shock.

Supporting her with an arm around her shoulders, he wrapped the blanket around her, then tucked it close to her body to help hold in the warmth. "Don't worry about it now, miss," he gently instructed. "You've had a nasty knock to your head. Just try to relax and we'll start from the beginning. Can you tell me your name?"

She looked at him and Brady felt something twist in his gut as he watched her lips tremble with fear and uncertainty. He'd never seen a woman look so lost and vulnerable and the protective side of him ached to reassure her, yet the lawman in him yanked those emotions back and ordered him to remember that his first priority was doing his job.

"I…no! Oh, God help me, I don't know my name!"

Over the years, Brady had learned that people who found themselves in trouble with the law oftentimes conveniently forgot their identities. That could be the case with this gray-eyed gal, but he didn't think she was acting. The shock on her face looked far too genuine.

Before he could decide how to reply to her anguished

plea, Hank walked up carrying nothing but a flashlight. Brady rose from his squat to talk to his partner.

"Nothing, Brady. Maybe we'll find something after daylight."

With a pointed glance at the blanket-wrapped woman, Brady gently elbowed Hank in the ribs and the two men walked a short distance away before stopping to converse in low voices.

"She's claiming she doesn't know who she is or where she is," Brady told him. "I'm thinking she has a heck of a concussion. It might be tomorrow before we find out what took place."

Frowning, Hank glanced over his shoulder at the injured woman. "Yeah. But she could be lying. Especially if there was a drug deal gone wrong. By tomorrow, she might lawyer up and decide not to tell us anything."

Brady's lips stretched into a grim line. He wasn't buying that scenario. He'd sensed something innocent about the woman. No doubt Hank would laugh at that notion, so Brady kept the opinion to himself. "Let's hope that doesn't happen."

"Is she Apache? Maybe she's from the res."

"No. She's white. Somewhere in her mid-twenties, I'd say."

Hank shook his head with disbelief. "Boy, oh, boy. And I thought this was going to be a boring night."

Brady slapped him on the shoulder. "You'd better get down to the highway. The ambulance ought to be here soon."

Forty-five minutes later, the ambulance had picked up the injured woman and carried her to Sierra General Hospital in Ruidoso. Brady and Hank arrived directly behind the emergency vehicle and followed the paramedics as they pushed the injured woman through the swishing doors.

Once they were inside the building, Hank said, "Guess we'd better give Admitting what information we have. But that's not a heck of a lot."

Brady's expression was rueful. "We have nothing but white female. Black hair, gray eyes, mid-twenties. They'll have to admit her as a Jane Doe."

As Brady and his partner paused in the middle of the corridor, two nurses hurried out and ordered the paramedics to take the patient farther down the hallway. As he watched the gurney and medical attendants make a sharp left and disappeared from view, Brady had the oddest urge to follow. He wanted to see for himself that the woman was going to be okay, that the nurses and doctors did everything they could to alleviate her pain and fears.

The urge was totally out of character for Brady and made him feel foolish. He'd always made it a policy to never let his emotions get tangled up with his job. It was easier that way. Easier to go home at night and forget the victims who'd been battered or robbed or abused. As a deputy, his job wasn't to fix personal problems, but to put criminals away so that no one else might be harmed.

Sure, when a young child was involved, there wasn't an officer on the force who wasn't emotionally affected. But the woman he'd found on the road tonight was hardly a child and what happened to her next shouldn't be on Brady's mind.

"Hey, Brady, you here on official business tonight? Or just to see your sister?"

At the sound of the female voice, Brady turned to see Andrea, a nurse who often worked the night shift in emergency.

"Bridget is working tonight?" he asked.

Brady's sister was a medical doctor with a very busy practice. She wasn't a hospital resident, but if any of her patients needed hospitalization she treated them here at Sierra General. If he could find her, he might be able to talk her in to taking over Jane Doe's case.

The tall, blonde nurse nodded. "I saw her a few minutes ago. She had some sort of emergency with a patient on the third floor."

Brady turned to his partner. "Can you deal with admitting her on your own?"

Hank shrugged. "Sure. Why?"

At that moment a male nurse at the front desk called to Andrea and as she quickly excused herself, Brady told the deputy, "I'm going to look for my sister."

Hank's brown brows pulled together to form a puzzled frown. "Bridget?" he asked blankly. "Why in heck do you need to see her right now? Your family having problems you haven't told me about?"

Brady had two brothers, three sisters, parents and a grandmother. And, except for one sister, they all lived in the same house on the Diamond D Ranch. Among that many relatives there were always problems arising, but thankfully usually minor ones.

"No, Hank. No problems!" Trotting toward the elevator, Brady said over his shoulder, "And don't run off to the coffee shop until I get back!"

On the third floor, Brady stepped off the elevator and headed to the nearest nurse's station. But before he reached the post, he spotted Bridget striding toward him.

When the petite redhead reached his side, she looked at him with faint alarm. "Brady! What are you doing here? Nothing is wrong with the family, is it?"

"Relax. As far as I know everyone is okay. I'm here on business."

Looping her arm through his, his sister pulled him to one side of the wide corridor so as not to clog the pathway. "Oh, I hope it's not a domestic battery," she said quickly. "I hate to hear about those victims, much less see them in the hospital."

Removing a gray Stetson from his head, Brady raked a hand through thick, tawny-colored waves. "Actually, I'm not sure what this woman is a victim of. Hank and I found her on a back mountain road a few miles from Picacho. The paramedics just brought her in a few minutes ago. She's had sort of trauma to the head. And I was…hoping you'd take a look at her."

His sister frowned. "Isn't one of the emergency doctors dealing with her?"

Brady felt like an idiot. The hospital was full of competent doctors and no doubt Gray Eyes would get the best of care. That should be enough for any patient. So why was he trying to garner her more attention?

"Yes. She's…being treating now. But I thought—well, I'd just feel better if you'd stop in and look at her."

"Who is it?" Bridget quickly questioned. "A friend? Someone we know?"

Shaking his head, he said, "Never seen her before. She doesn't know who she is."

Bridget started to ask another question, but at that moment, a small group of people walking past them called greetings to his sister, momentarily distracting her from their conversation.

"Sorry, Brady," she said, once the medical personnel had moved on down the corridor and away from them. "You were saying—"

"She's blank, Brita. Not her name, where she was or why. Nothing. And no ID to tell us."

A thoughtful frown crossed his sister's face. "A head injury, you say?"

Brady nodded. "A bad gash near her temple."

Suddenly she patted his forearm in a placating way. "I think Dr. Richmond is on emergency call this evening. He's certainly capable of taking care of this type of injury."

"I'm sure he is. But she'll have to be handed over to the care of a permanent physician. And she doesn't know anyone and—"

Sensing his urgency, she released a sigh of surrender. "Okay, Brady, okay. I'll take a look. But mind you, when her family steps forward and requests another doctor, I'll be gone. Understand?"

Smiling with relief, he clasped a loving arm around her shoulders and squeezed. "Did you know that you're my favorite sister?"

She shot him a tired look. "Yeah. Your favorite is the one you happen to be with at the moment. And do I need to remind you of the messes you've gotten me into? That time—"

"We don't have time to go into my transgressions now, sis," Brady interrupted as he urged his sister toward the nearest elevator. "I promise I'll make everything up to you. Someday."

The cubicle behind the plain beige curtain was cold and smelled faintly of disinfectant. Standing a few feet away, at the foot of the narrow, railed bed, a middle-aged doctor with dark blond hair and black rimmed glasses was scratching notes on a clipboard, while barking orders at the attending nurse.

Since arriving in the emergency unit, she'd been stripped of her boots and clothing, sponged clean and dressed in a blue cotton gown that tied at the back. The doctor had poked and prodded, asked her questions that she couldn't answer and generally done little to assuage her fears.

Now that he'd ended his examination and was conversing with the nurse, her mind vacillated between sheer panic and a pit of total emptiness.

Scans. Sutures. Neurological tests. The medical words she managed to catch here and there made little to no sense to her.

Oh, God, who was she? Where was she? The questions pounded through her head, adding to the horrible throb in her right temple.

Thinking was like bouncing herself off a black wall where there was no door or crack of light to lead her either forward or backward. Other than waking up to see a deputy sheriff hovering over her, there was nothing in her mind, except icy, paralyzing fear.

She tried to push the terror back and keep from sobbing as the doctor exited the cubicle and the young nurse with a kind face bent over her. The name tag pinned to the left side of her chest said her name was Lilly.

"All right, miss," she said warmly. "Let's get some pain medication started and then we'll see about taking you down to radiology. When that's done someone will come around to put some stitches in your scalp."

During the ambulance ride, the paramedics had started an intravenous drip. Now the nurse simply pushed a syringe full of medication into the tube already affixed to her hand.

"Why am I going to radiology?"

"To take pictures of your skull and brain," the nurse replied. "Dr. Richmond needs to see if you have internal injuries."

"Oh." She didn't want pictures or stitches, she wanted

to scream. She wanted her memory back. "Will that take long? The tests?"

"No," the nurse assured her. "They won't hurt, either."

She closed her eyes. "Um—the deputy who found me. Is he here?"

Lilly answered, "I saw Hank Ridell out in the corridor a few minutes ago. Is that who you mean?"

She opened her eyes to see the nurse was writing something on the chart the doctor had left behind.

"No. His name was Donovan, I think. He was tall and had on a gray hat and he had a little scar right here." She touched a finger to a spot on her cheekbone near her eye.

Lilly suddenly smiled a knowing smile. "Oh. That's Brady. He's the chief deputy of Lincoln County. And considered quite a catch by most of the young women around here."

The pain medication was beginning to course rapidly through her bloodstream, easing the pounding in her head. "Including you?" she asked the nurse.

Lilly blushed and laughed. "No. I have a boyfriend. Besides, I'm not in Brady Donovan's league." She placed the chart in a holder at the foot of the bed, then studied her more closely. "Did you need to talk with the deputy for some reason?"

There were a thousand things she wanted to ask the man, things that might help jar her memory. But that wasn't entirely the reason she wanted to see the deputy again. He'd been nice and gentle. He'd held her with strong hands and soothed her with his low voice. At some point during their wait for the ambulance, he'd become her light in a heavy fog. She'd not wanted to leave him and now she fervently wished he was back by her side.

"I would like to speak with him. If you think that's possible."

Smiling, Lilly winked at her. "While you're in radiology I'll do my best to find him."

The nurse quickly swished out the door and as she watched her go, she desperately prayed the woman would find the deputy.

Her world had gone crazy and he was the only person, the only thing her memory had to go back to. She was totally and utterly lost. And without Deputy Donovan, she didn't know if she'd ever be able to find her way back home.

Chapter Two

More than an hour later, Brady and Hank were sitting in the hospital coffee shop, finishing off huge slices of pie when Bridget walked up to their table.

Shaking her head, she looked at the crumbs on their plates. "Looks like both of you are really worried about good nutrition," she said wryly.

"Pecan pie must be good for you or the hospital wouldn't serve it, right?" Hank asked.

"Wrong. But it looks delicious," she said with a weary sigh.

Immediately, Hank jumped from his seat and pulled out a chair for her.

"Did you see our Jane Doe?" Brady questioned before she had time to get comfortable.

The doctor thanked Hank, then pushed a hand through

her tumbled hair. "I did," she said to Brady. "And I've become her doctor. For the time being."

"I'm glad. So what about her condition?" Brady questioned.

His sister frowned at him. "I can't give you details, Brady. You know that's invading a patient's privacy."

Brady muttered a curse word under his breath. For the past two hours he'd not been able to think about anything except the gray-eyed woman he'd held in his arms. Now his sister wanted to act all professional with him.

"Damn it, Brita, just tell me—is she going to get better? Is she going to be able to remember? Tell us who she is?"

Bridget studied him keenly, and then glanced pointedly at Hank. "What has he done, had a love-at-first-sight experience?"

Hank grinned. "You mean another one?"

Normally Brady liked to joke. In fact, Fiona Donovan had often called him her most lighthearted child, full of happiness and humor. But at the moment he wasn't feeling anything of the sort. In fact, he was getting a tad angry at both his sister and his partner.

Scowling, Brady muttered to the both of them, "I'm not in the mood for this!"

Seeing he was serious, Bridget relented. "Okay, brother, I'll be straightforward. Your Jane Doe will get better. The good news is that physically she's fine. She wasn't raped, and aside from some bruising on her arms and legs she isn't seriously injured. As for her memory, how long that might take is a question I can't answer."

"Are you kiddin' me?"

Reaching across the table, she patted the back of his hand. "No. Medicine is not always an exact science. And head injuries are sometimes tricky. She might remember everything in the next few minutes, years from now, something in-between, or never."

The picture of awful uncertainty his sister was painting hit Brady like a fist to his mouth. No matter the circumstances that caused the injury, the woman didn't deserve this.

"Isn't there something you can do to make her remember? Give her some sort of drug?"

"Trust me, Brady. If she doesn't improve quickly, I'll be calling in a specialist. But since she's a ward of the county, cost has to be considered—there's just so much the hospital will allow. And quit staring at me like you expect me to perform some sort of miracle. I'm just a doctor."

Hank suddenly interjected, "Look, Brady, it might be that we find her ID when we return to the scene in the morning. Who knows, we might even find an abandoned vehicle in the area."

Brady wished they didn't have to wait until daylight to return to the scene. He wanted answers now. But the department's manpower was already stretched across the enormous county. To bring in searchlights would be costly, time-consuming and perhaps even worthless in the long run.

"Yeah," Brady agreed. "Let's hope."

Bridget suddenly squeezed his fingers and he glanced back at his sister.

"I almost forgot—she's asking for you."

Brady's mouth fell open. "Me?"

Bridget's smile was wry. "Yes, you. She wants to see you. I expect the meds we've given her will be putting her to sleep soon, so you'd better get going."

Gray Eyes wanted to see him? The news didn't just stun Brady, it pleased him in the goofiest sort of way and he hurriedly scraped back his chair.

"I'll be back in a few minutes, Hank." Rising to his feet,

he pulled out his wallet and tossed several bills at Hank. "Here. Buy Bridget a piece of pie. She looks hungry."

He headed toward the plate glass door leading out of the coffee shop when suddenly his sister's voice called out to him.

"Brady, where are you going?"

Frowning with frustration, he glanced over his shoulder. "Where do you think I'm going?" he asked impatiently.

With a shake of her head, she looked drolly over to Hank, then back to her brother. "I don't know. There are nearly five hundred rooms in this hospital. Don't you think you need the number to find her?"

If Brady didn't feel like an idiot before, he certainly did now and he was glad he was standing a few feet away from the table. Otherwise Hank could easily see the red on his face.

"All right," he conceded. "I wasn't thinking. What's the number?"

"Two-twelve. And Brady, be easy," she warned.

A lazy smile crossed Brady's face. "Don't worry, sis. If there's one thing I'm good at, it's handling women. Especially damsels in distress."

When a knock sounded on the door, she didn't bother to open her eyes. For the past thirty minutes the nurses had been coming and going from the hospital room like ants on a picnic blanket. She expected the footsteps she heard approaching her bed belonged to yet another nurse who was there to take her blood pressure for the umpteenth time.

"Excuse me, miss. It's Deputy Donovan. Do you feel like talking?"

The sound of his voice set her heart to pounding and her eyes popped open to see him standing near the head of the bed. His gray hat was in his hand and beneath the dim lighting she could see rusty-gold hair waving thickly about his head, tanned features molded in a sober expression.

He was a young man, she decided. Somewhere in his late twenties or early thirties. *Handsome* was not the word to come to her mind as she studied him more closely. But *rugged* and *sexy* certainly did. Sharp cheekbones, a thrusting chin, hazel green eyes and a full lower lip merged together to form one strong face.

Suddenly feeling as weak as a puny kitten, she cleared her throat and tried to speak in a normal voice. Instead, it came out raspy. "Thank you for coming, Deputy Donovan."

A faint smile tilted the corner of his lips and her gaze was drawn to his mouth and the dimple marking his left cheek.

"My pleasure," he said. "How are you feeling?"

That voice. It was her first memory of anything and she clung to it like a child with a blanket. "Lousy. But better."

"I'm glad to hear it. Hopefully, you'll be right as rain real soon."

She swallowed as hopeless emotions thickened her throat. "Doctor Donovan was very positive about that. She…told me that she's your sister."

His smile deepened. "That's right. We're from a big family. We all live together in a big ranch house."

Family. Parents. Siblings. Did she have any? And if she did, where were they? Nearby? Far away? Maybe she had no one. Oh, God, let her remember, she prayed.

Her gaze fell from his face and settled on the folds of her blue hospital gown. "No one here at the hospital seems to recognize me. I…don't know if I have any…family."

His hand was suddenly touching her shoulder and the warmth from it spread through her, easing the chill that she couldn't seem to shake in spite of the extra blankets the nurses had spread over her.

"If you do, we'll find them. Trust me on that."

He sounded so confident, so firm in his conviction, that she had to believe him. Her gaze fluttered back to his face. "I can't remember anything about the place where you found me. Was it near a house or anything?"

"No. The road is a back road that leads into the mountains. Ranchers use it to move their sheep and cattle from one range to another and hunters travel it during open season. That's about all. The nearest house to where we found you is probably six or seven miles away."

She shook her head with dismay. "What could I have been doing there? Was there a car? Anything?"

"Not that we've found yet. We'll be examining your clothes and scouring the area in the morning. If you left anything behind, we'll find it."

She drew in a deep breath and let it out. She was exhausted and her body was screaming for sleep, yet she fought the fogginess settling over her. She wanted to be with this man a little longer, absorb the security he lent her.

"If I—don't remember, is there much you can do to find out who I am?"

His fingers tightened reassuringly on her shoulder. "Don't worry about that tonight. Everything is going to be all right. I promise."

He was trying to make her feel better and oddly enough, he was. "I don't even have a name for you to call me," she said, then tried to laugh at the ridiculousness of her situation. "I guess I'm a Jane Doe, aren't I? But please don't call me that. I never liked the name Jane that much."

His brows arched. "How do you know something like that without remembering?"

"I—well, I don't know why I dislike the name. I just

know that I do," she said with faint surprise. "But I guess you're right. Subconsciously I must be remembering something."

Brady had never wanted to take anyone in his arms more than he did this woman at this very moment. She looked lost and wounded and utterly beautiful. And everything inside him wanted to make her better.

"See," he said gently, "your memory will all come back and then you can tell me your real name. But for now let's give you another one. What would you like to be called?"

One hand lifted, then fell helplessly back to the bed covers. "It doesn't matter."

"It must have," he said with an easy chuckle. "You didn't want to be called Jane."

A tiny smile curved her lips and he felt instantly better.

"Well. That's different," she said. "I don't want to be a Jane. I want to be someone real."

"All right. Then I'm going to call you…" He thought for a moment, then smiled with satisfaction. "Lass."

Even though her gray eyes were full of sleep, he could see surprise flicker in their drowsy debts.

"Lass," she repeated as though testing the name on her tongue. "Why?"

Brady couldn't stop his fingers from moving to her forehead and gently pushing a strand of shiny black hair away from the bruised flesh near her eye. Did this woman have a husband somewhere, he wondered? A husband that often touched her this very same way?

During the time the two of them had spent waiting for the ambulance to arrive, Brady had studied her hands. From a professional standpoint, he'd wanted to see if there had been defensive wounds on her hands or traces of flesh or hair beneath her fingernails from fighting off an attacker.

From a personal position, he'd wanted to see if she was wearing a wedding band or engagement ring.

Except for a bit of grime on her palms, her hands had been clean. But that might not mean she was single. Her ring could have been stolen or she could have simply not been wearing it when she'd left home. Or not had one on for very long—not long enough to get a tan line or callus.

"Well, Lassie got lost lots of times," he reasoned, "and she always found her way back home to her family. Then everyone was happy again. That's the way it's going to be with you, Lass."

She reached for his hand and as her fingers curled loosely around his, her eyelids drifted downward

"Lass," she repeated sleepily. "That's very pretty. Thank you, Deputy."

Brady was about to tell her that no thanks were needed, but at that moment the muscles in her face went lax and the fingers wrapped around his lost their grip and dropped to the white sheet covering her body.

She'd fallen asleep and it was time for him to go, he realized. Yet he lingered beside the bed, unable to tear his gaze away from the woman.

She was smaller than he'd first estimated, but her arms appeared toned and muscled. No doubt the rest of her was as fit, he thought. This told him she wasn't someone who sat around all day. She either worked at something that required manual labor or she made frequent visits to the gym. Her hair was shiny and well cared for, the straight ends trimmed to blunt precision. Pale pink polish covered her short, well-manicured nails and her satiny smooth skin looked as though it had been pampered since birth.

She definitely wasn't blue collar, he thought. Along with her grooming habits, there were also the earrings attached to her lobes. If he was a betting man, he'd wager the glittering stones circling the chunks of turquoise were real diamonds. A fact that only added to her strange circumstance.

If someone had whacked her in the head to rob her, why hadn't the thief taken the pricey jewelry? No, something else had gone down with this little, lost lassie and he was going to do his damnedest to find out.

His thoughts were interrupted by a faint knock on the door and Brady turned from the bed just as his sister stepped into the room.

"I think she's gone to sleep," Brady said, hoping he didn't look as sheepish as he felt. "And I...was just about to leave."

Bridget peered around his shoulder at her sleeping patient, then back at him. "I'm on my way home. I wanted to see if she recalled anything that might be helpful."

Brady shook his head. "No."

"Well, it will come." She rose on tiptoes and planted a kiss on his cheek. "Good night, Brady. And don't look worried. You've always been good at your job. You'll figure out where this Jane Doe belongs."

"She's not Jane Doe. I've named her Lass and that's what she's going to go by. Until—well, until she remembers or we figure out her real identity."

Bridget appeared amused. "Lass, eh? That ought to fit right in with our Irish brood. What are you doing, making plans to adopt her?"

"Damn it, Brita, that remark was uncalled for."

Frustrated, he stepped around his sister and headed out of the room. Bridget followed closely on his heels and once they were out in the corridor, she grabbed him by the arm.

"Okay. I'm sorry," she apologized. "I was only trying to lighten things up with a little humor. What's the matter with you tonight, anyway? You're as prickly as Grandma's rose bushes."

Brady sighed. He honestly didn't know what was eating at him. He was thankful, very thankful, that he and Hank had just happened to be traveling the road where Lass had lain unconscious. If not, well, he didn't want to think about the outcome. And yet, the whole ordeal had shaken him, affected him like nothing he'd dealt with before.

"You're right." Pinching the bridge of his nose, he momentarily closed his eyes. "I guess…it's not every day that we find someone left on the side of the road for dead. I keep thinking, if that was you I'd want someone to do everything they could to help you."

Bridget rubbed his forearm with understanding. "I always thought you were too soft-hearted for this job," she said gently.

A dry smile curved his lips as he opened his eyes and looked down at her. "Hell, other than Grandma, you're probably the only one in the family who thinks I have a heart."

Her soft laugh was full of affection. "That's because they don't know you like we do."

Were his sister and grandmother the only ones who realized he was more than a lawman, covering his heart with a bullet proof vest? How did Lass see him?

Forget that last question, Brady. How Gray Eyes sees you is irrelevant. She's just a part of your job. Nothing more. Nothing less.

The next morning, Brady and Hank and two other deputies returned to the mountain road near Picacho to search the area for clues. Thankfully, the day was bright and no rain had fallen during the night to wash away evidence. But unfortunately, they found nothing, except a crumpled betting ticket from Ruidoso Downs Race-track. The twenty-dollar bet, found lying against a clump of sage, about a hundred yards down the road from Lass, had been for a trifecta on the fifth race of yesterday's card. After a quick call to the track, Brady had learned that the ticket was worthless, so there was no other record of it.

But the money, or lack of it, was inconsequential at the moment, Brady figured. The main question was why the ticket was here on this back road where there was nothing but wilderness? Had a group of party-goers from the track driven out here just to find an isolated place to whoop it up? Teenagers might do something that foolish. But teen-agers couldn't wager. And Lass wasn't a teen.

None of it made sense to Brady or his partner as they exchanged speculations.

"Maybe Lass was at the track yesterday and the ticket fell out of her pocket when she whammed her head," Hank said as the two men stood in the middle of the quiet dirt road.

"Or when someone whammed it for her," Brady said grimly. "We'll post a few pictures of her at the track. We might get lucky and one of the clerks working the betting cages will recognize her."

Last night, after Brady and Hank had left the hospital, they'd driven the thirty-mile trip to their headquarters in Carrizozo to finish the remainder of their shift. Before he'd gone home, Brady had looked through as many missing cases that could possibly be tied to the area and he'd come up with nothing that matched Lass's description. No calls had come in to the sheriff's office reporting anyone missing. Nor had there been any calls for domestic disputes, robberies or assaults. Other than the incident with Lass, the only thing that had gone on was a few public intoxication and DUI arrests. Like Hank had said, last night had been as quiet as a sleeping cat.

This morning, after a lengthy meeting, Sheriff Hamilton had turned the entire case over to Brady and now as he scanned the rough terrain beyond the smoky lens of his sunglasses, he was feeling a heavy weight on his shoulders. For years now, Ethan Hamilton had been his mentor, even his hero. He never wanted to let the man down. Yet incredibly, it was Lass and her pleading face that was weighing on him the most.

Hank's voice suddenly interrupted Brady's deep thoughts. "It's too bad we couldn't have found her in the daylight. We might have been able to pick up on more footprints. Looks like most of them were blown away with last night's wind."

"No one ever said our job was supposed to be easy," Brady replied as he continued to study the area around them.

The trees and vegetation weren't exactly thick, but there was enough juniper and pine for a person to hide or get lost in. Not that either scenario applied to Lass, he thought. But his gut feeling kept telling him that she'd come out of the mountains and then ended up at the road's edge, rather than the other way around.

"I think I'll have a talk with Johnny Chino and see if he'll come have a look at things," Brady said after a moment. "It might help us to know what direction Lass came from before she ended up in the ditch."

Hank tossed him a skeptical glance. "Good luck. Johnny hasn't done any tracking since—well, not for years."

Brady sighed. The Apache tracker was one of the best. But for a long time now the man had turned his back on a job that had once taken him all over the southwest. Brady didn't exactly know what sort of personal demons the tracker was carrying around, but he figured working again would be the best way for Johnny to get rid of them.

"He might do it for me. We've been friends since we were kids."

"Like I said, good luck," Hank muttered.

She was running through inky darkness. Stumbling over rocks and fallen branches. Her breaths were gasps of fire, burning her lungs and stabbing her chest with searing pain. Somewhere, far in front of her, she would find light and safety. If only she could keep running. If only…

"Lass? It's Dr. Donovan. Wake up and talk with me."

The firm voice penetrated the dark terror around her and Lass jerked awake with a jolt to see Deputy Donovan's sister standing next to her bed.

"Oh! It's you, Doctor." Shoving a handful of disheveled hair off her face, Lass eased to a sitting position in the bed and blinked her eyes. Her whole body felt damp and her heart was pounding with lingering fear. "I guess I dozed off. I must have been dreaming or maybe I was trying to remember—I don't know."

The redheaded doctor studied her closely. "Do you remember your dream?"

Nodding, Lass shivered. "I was running in the dark. Away from something. And I was terrified. That's all I know."

The doctor pulled out a pin light and flashed it in both of Lass's eyes. "Mmm. That's a common nightmare. It could be a result of the trauma you've gone through or you could be remembering something that happened. Hard to say. In any case, I'm happy to report that your scans have been read and there are no fractures to your skull or any other major brain damage. You have a garden variety concussion and it should go away in the next few days. And it's a positive sign to see that your short-term memory is working. You obviously remember that I'm your doctor and you remembered your dream."

The doctor put the pin light away and placed a stethoscope to Lass's chest. Once she'd listened to her satisfaction, then hung the instrument back around her neck, Lass asked, "What about the rest of my memory? I keep working my mind, trying to think past last night. I can't."

The doctor gently patted her shoulder. "I'm hopeful that once the swelling in your brain starts to recede and everything begins to heal itself, your memory will return. But in the meantime, I'm going to have a specialist come in this afternoon and speak with you."

"A specialist?" Lass asked warily. "What kind of specialist?"

Dr. Donovan's smile was meant to be reassuring. "A psychiatrist."

Lass stared at her in horror. "Do you…think I'm crazy? Oh, God, I never thought about that! I might have been institutionalized and wandered away. Maybe I hurt someone and they put me away! I—"

With each word that passed her lips, Lass grew more and more agitated.

"Lass," the doctor said gently. "You need to stop this. I can assure you that no one here has detected any sort of mental illness. The psychiatrist will simply talk to you and perhaps help coax some of your memories to return. That's all."

Lass's shoulders slumped with relief. She didn't know why her thoughts kept running toward such negative speculations. Had she been in some sort of trouble? Criminal trouble?

What a stupid question, Lass. Trouble might as well be written across your forehead. Anyone who's found on the

side of the road with a head bashed is bound to be con-
nected to some sort of trouble. What do you think you were
doing out there in the mountains in the middle of the night?
Admiring the wildflowers?

Swallowing, she forced the troubling questions aside
and tried to focus on the doctor. "So—how much longer
will I have to be in the hospital?" she asked.

"If no complications pop up, I'll be releasing you
tomorrow." Dr. Donovan smiled with encouragement. "As
for this morning, the nurses are going to come in and help
you shower and dress. And if you're steady enough on
your feet, you can move around somewhat. But I don't
want you overdoing it, okay?"

Lass agreed and the doctor continued to give her a few
more orders before she finally said goodbye and left the room.

Once she was gone, Lass let out a heavy sigh as her gaze
surveyed her surroundings. For the moment, the small, stark
room was her home. But tomorrow she'd be leaving. To
where? Where was her home? Oh, God, if she only knew.

Chapter Three

Later that afternoon while Hank questioned workers at the racetrack, Brady drove to the hospital to check on Lass. From the report Bridget had given him earlier this morning, the young woman's memory was still a blank. But he was hoping each hour that passed would bring her closer to recalling her identity and, moreover, what had happened to her the night before.

On the second floor, he stepped off the elevator and turned right in the direction of Lass's room, but before he could get past the nurse's desk, a young woman with long brown hair wrapped in a knot atop her head waved and called to him.

"Hey, Brady! Are you going to the concert next weekend at the rodeo arena?"

He paused as the nurse came rushing up to him. Miranda was a sweet girl he'd once dated a few times, but it had quickly become obvious to both of them that she'd wanted more than just a good time together. Thankfully, she'd understood that he wasn't looking for a permanent partner and they'd parted on friendly terms.

He shook his head. "Not unless I have to provide security. And right now the city police are planning on handling it."

With Lass's case thrown on his plate, he wasn't going to have much free time in the coming days. Unless, she miraculously recovered, or someone showed up to identify her.

"Guess you're busy with the Jane Doe thing," she commented. "I think I ought to tell you that most of the hospital stopped by to see her. We'd been hoping someone would recognize her, but nobody does."

"Thanks for letting me know, Miranda. I appreciate the attempt."

Miranda grimaced with regret. "Poor thing. And she's so pretty, too. What will happen to her? I mean, if she doesn't remember? I guess she'll have to go to one of those shelters." Miranda shuddered with distaste. "Maybe you'll figure it out, Brady, before that happens."

He nodded and she quickly excused herself as the phone on the nurse's desk began to shrill loudly. Brady hurried on to Lass's room and as he went, Miranda's suggestion plagued him. To think of Lass thrown in a rescue mission or a shelter for battered women sickened him. And whether she remembered or not, he couldn't let it happen.

After a short knock on her door, he stepped inside the room and was pleasantly surprised to find her dressed and sitting in a cushioned chair positioned near the room's only window.

"Well, you look much better than the last time I saw you," he greeted. "How are you feeling?"

She was wearing the clothes he'd found her in and though they were smudged with dirt in spots, they made her look far more normal than the hideous hospital gown. Her long hair had been pulled back from her face and fastened at her nape with a rubber band. The style exposed her swollen eye yet at the same time revealed the long, lovely line of her neck.

"Stronger," she answered. "And my head doesn't hurt nearly as much."

He moved across the room, then stopped a couple of feet from her chair. The late afternoon sun slanted a golden ray across her lap and cast a sheen to her crow-black hair. Except for her cheeks, her skin was as pale as milk and he found himself tempering the urge to reach over and touch it, test its softness with the pads of his fingers.

Clearing his throat, he said, "That's good. Bridget says you're on the mend."

Her features tightened. "Did she also tell you that she sent a psychiatrist to talk with me?"

Brady looked at her in surprise. "No. But I'm glad. I told her to help you in every way that she could. Obviously she's not going to leave any stone unturned." He took a seat on the edge of the narrow bed. "So what did the psychiatrist have to say?"

She rubbed her hands nervously down the thighs of her jeans. "Well, that I'm not crazy or anything like that."

Brady grinned. "I could have told you that much."

She darted a sober glance at him. "He also said that I might not be remembering because I'm afraid to remember."

Folding his arms against his chest, Brady studied her with interest. "Like a psychosomatic thing," he said.

Her brows arched with surprise. "Why, yes. How did you know that? Have you studied medicine, too?"

Brady chuckled. "No. I left that to my sisters. I'm a lawman. I study human characters. And believe me, seeing people under stress and in trouble makes for a good psychology class."

Dropping her head, she let out a heavy breath. "Well, I've not remembered anything. Unless you count the dream I had. And that didn't tell me much. Except that I was running in the dark and whatever was behind me was scaring the living daylights out of me." She looked up at him, her expression twisted with something close to agony. "Your sister says she's going to release me from the hospital tomorrow. What does that mean, Deputy Donovan? What will happen to me then?"

He swiftly shook his head. "I'd be pleased if you'd call me Brady. And don't worry—we'll find some place nice for you to stay until we can get a fix on where you really belong."

Suddenly it dawned on him that she had nothing but the clothes on her back. No handbag with all the little necessities women carried with them. No cell phone filled with numbers of friends and family that she might call for help. No credit cards or checkbook or any sort of means to provide for herself. She was totally dependent and, at the moment, looking straight at him for answers.

She didn't make any sort of reply to his comment and Brady figured there wasn't much she could say. She was at the mercy of the county and what it could provide for her. Unless he stepped in, he thought, as his mind suddenly jumped forward. Since his older sister, Maura, had married Quint Cantrell, her room had become empty. Brady's home, the Diamond D Ranch, was a huge place with plenty of space for a guest. What would his family think if he showed up with Lass? He and his sister Dallas had always been guilty of picking up strays that needed a home. Well,

Lass was no different, he rationalized. She needed a home in the worst kind of way.

"Thank you, Brady. I guess… Well, you know the old saying—beggars can't be choosers. I'm obviously in that position now."

Changing the subject for the moment, he suddenly asked, "Did someone from the sheriff's department come by to take your picture?"

She nodded. "Yes. A lady. She said you were going to be putting it on posters around town and posting it on the Internet."

"That's right. We also plan to put it in the area papers. See if that will turn up any leads. But in the meantime, you'll need some help. A place to stay, clothes and things like that. I'm thinking—" His gaze zeroed in on hers. "How would you feel about staying at my home? Until we get your problem worked out?"

Her gray eyes narrowed with something like mistrust. "I don't understand. I'm not your responsibility. I mean, I know that you and your partner are the ones who found me, but that doesn't mean—"

She broke off as he quickly shook his head. "Look, Lass, I'll be frank. I don't think you'd much like living in a shelter. You wouldn't have much privacy and some of the women there—they're dealing with some pretty bad problems."

Her lips quivered. "And I'm not?"

He tried to give her the same sort of smile Brady's mother gave him when he was fretting over an issue that was beyond his control. "As of right now, Lass, the only problem we're certain that you have is amnesia. And the way I see it, you could've had a whole lot worse things happen to you."

"Maybe I did. And we just don't know. Maybe I'd bring

trouble to your family and—" Her words abruptly trailing off, she shook her head and rose slowly from her chair. "I don't want to be a burden or a…problem. Thank you for your kind offer, Brady, but I can't accept."

Feeling ridiculously squashed, he watched her move to the window and stare out at the small manicured lawn at the back of the building. To one side of the grassy area, a patio had been constructed and offered a group of comfortable lawn chairs to visitors who needed a break from the confines of a sterile hospital room.

At the moment a young woman with two small children in hand was strolling among the potted desert plants that adorned the patio. Lass appeared to be focused on the sight of the playful youngsters and Brady wondered if she might have children of her own, children that were missing their mother. For some reason he didn't like the image of her being a mother, or a wife. And yet, he realized that if she did have a family waiting for her somewhere, she needed to get back to them as quickly as possible. More importantly, it was his job to see that she was reunited with her loved ones.

"I assure you, Lass, you're not going to cause trouble. And even if you did, we Donovans know how to deal with trouble. Besides, you being on the ranch would be a big help to me."

A frown puckered her forehead as she pulled her attention away from the children and over to him. "Really? How is that?"

"Well, until we discover your identity, you're going to have to keep in close contact with the sheriff's department. Since I'm in charge of your case that means me. And having you on the Diamond D will make it convenient for the two of us to work together."

"The Diamond D," she repeated thoughtfully. "I think I recall you saying last night that you lived on a ranch. Your family raises cattle?"

"Horses," he explained. "Racehorses."

"Oh." The frown on her face deepened. "What do you do with racehorses around here? The nurses tell me that this is a relatively small town. Most of the major tracks are on the east and west coasts."

Rising from the bed, he joined her at the window. As he rested his hip on the wide seal, he studied her keenly. "If you remember such things as that, then apparently a part of your memory is working. As for our horses, we—or I should say my brother Liam—hauls them cross-country to race. But Ruidoso has a track and it's becoming significant in its own right. It's the home of the Million Dollar Futurity that takes place every Labor Day."

"I see," she murmured, then thoughtfully shook her head. "I wonder why I knew about the major tracks? Perhaps I'm connected to the business in some way. But I'm…only guessing. It's just a feeling I have. Not a memory."

Brady's mind was leaping in all direction as he attempted to connect what dots he had. "I don't know if this means anything, Lass, but one of the deputies found a wagering ticket from Ruidoso Downs not far from where you were found. The track, betting, horses—do any of those things ring a bell?"

She stared out the window for long moments, then with a groan of defeat, pressed a hand to her forehead. "I'm sorry, Brady. When I try to think of anything personal, it's all a blank. And the harder I try to think, the more my head aches."

"Then don't try to think," he urged with concern. "Bridget would have my hide if she found out I'm making your condition worse."

Quickly, as though to reassure him, she reached out and touched his arm. "It's not your fault. Please don't think so. You're only trying to help me."

The touch of her hand on his bare forearm was as light as a butterfly and though her fingers were cool, Brady's reaction was just the opposite. Heat flowed along his arm as though he'd been touched by a torch, and for a moment he was lost for words, lost in the gray depths of her sad eyes.

"Don't worry about me, Lass. I've got a thick hide." At least, he'd believed he was tough-skinned, until she'd touched him. Dear Lord, he had to get out of here before he did something totally unprofessional. Like gather her into his arms and cuddle her against his chest. "And right now I have to get back to work."

Unable to tear his eyes away from her, he began to move backward toward the door.

"What about tomorrow?" she asked in bewilderment.

He flashed a smile. "Bridget will let me know when to be here to pick you up."

"But I—"

Placing a finger against his lips, he said, "I promise, my folks will be thrilled to have you."

And so would he, Brady silently admitted. But how long would it be before the thrill turned into a problem? Before good intentions turned bad?

Brady wasn't going to let himself think about those questions. Right now Lass needed him. And that was all that mattered.

The next morning Brady had been at his desk for over an hour when Sheriff Hamilton arrived at work. As the tall, dark-haired man sauntered through Brady's small work area, he stopped in his tracks and stared at his chief deputy.

"It's not even daylight yet. What are you doing here?"

Brady glanced up from his computer screen. Ethan Hamilton was a big man in stature and presence and held a lifelong connection to the area he served. Eleven years ago, when Roy Pardee had retired, Ethan had stepped into a pair of mighty big boots. Roy had been loved and revered, a living legend as far as citizens of the county were concerned and being the man's nephew had only made it harder for Ethan to prove himself. Down through the years he'd done that and more. He'd married the county judge, Penelope Parker, and they were now raising twin sons, Jake and Jase.

"I could say the same about you." Even though Ethan was clearly the boss, the two men were longtime friends and they conversed as such. Now Brady swiveled the rolling chair away from the desk and stood facing the sheriff. "Is something going on with you?"

"Penny's still feeling puny and she was up early," Ethan explained. "Once she gets up, I can't sleep."

"Again? Maybe you should take her to a doctor. See what's wrong with the woman," Brady suggested.

A slow smile spread across the sheriff's face. "I don't need to. She went to the doctor yesterday and he assured her everything would get back to normal—in seven months. Or as normal as it can be with another baby in the house."

Brady was stunned. Ethan and Penny's twins were nearly twelve years old. After all this time, he'd never figured the couple wanting more children. "Penny is…pregnant?"

"Yeah," he said with a beaming smile. "Isn't it great? We'd been wanting more children for a long time, but she's had health issues. Her having the twins was a miracle, so we figured it would be a second miracle if she could get pregnant again. We'd almost given up, but now it's happened and the doc says everything is going along fine."

The sheriff was a true family man and nothing made him happier than his wife and children. Brady could only wonder if he'd ever want to be that settled, that focused on one certain woman. So far he'd not found one that could hold his interest for more than a month, much less forever. Where women were concerned, Brady's mother accused him of being a selfish alpha male who expected too much from a lady. But Brady would hardly classify himself in those terms. He'd rather think of himself as smart and practical. And he was smart enough to know that he wasn't ready or willing to turn his life over to a woman. For that to happen, he'd have to be head over heels in love. And so far, that malady had never struck Brady.

Shaking the sheriff's hand heartily, Brady expressed his congratulations. "Wow! This must have been a pleasant surprise for the whole family! You must be walking on a cloud right about now!"

The sheriff chuckled. "The whole Murdock clan has kept the phone lines hot with the news. And me, well, I'm not even complaining about having to cook breakfast for me and the boys for the past week. Penny can't stand the smell of food early in the mornings. She won't even let me make coffee. And speaking of coffee—" he glanced over his shoulder to a corner where the coffeemaker was located "—has anyone made a pot yet?"

"Yeah. Me. I'll get us both a cup," Brady told him. "I need to talk with you."

"Fine. Bring it on to my office," he said. "I want to see if Dottie has left any notes on my desk."

Moments later, carrying two cups steaming with coffee,

Brady entered the sheriff's office and took a seat in front of the other man's desk.

"So," Ethan said as he sipped from the cup and rifled through the scraps of paper scattered in front of him, "you have something personal on your mind? Or business?"

Feeling sheepish and not really knowing why, Brady cleared his throat. "A little of both, I suppose. It's about the Jane Doe case. She's getting released from the hospital today. And I…plan on taking her out to the ranch."

Ethan's head shot up. "The Diamond D—?"

"That's right. Do you have any problems with that?"

The sheriff rubbed a finger along his jaw. "Well, I don't think there's any law against it. But I…wouldn't advise it, Brady. The county has places for people like her. They'll look out for her until we get this thing straightened out."

Frowning with disapproval, Brady leaned forward. "Sure. In that women's shelter down in Ruidoso. That wouldn't be good."

"Why not?"

Brady slowly sipped his coffee while he tried to gather all the legitimate excuses he could think of. "Well, it's right next to the mission for people with addiction problems."

"She won't have to mingle with those people."

Drawing in a deep breath, Brady tried again. "The women's shelter is small and they rarely have enough room to spare. Lass wouldn't have any privacy and she'd have to wear whatever she could find out of the charity box."

Ethan picked up another note and scanned the brief contents. "I could think of worse things."

Brady's jaw tightened. "She doesn't come from that sort of background, Ethan. She doesn't belong there."

The sheriff shot him a wry look, before he carefully sipped his coffee. "None of the other women belong there, either, Brady. Bad circumstances put them there. Just like the Jane—" He suddenly paused, his eyes narrowing on Brady's face. "Did I hear you call her 'Lass'? Has she remembered her name?"

Brady couldn't stop a wave of red heat from crawling up his neck and onto his face. "No. Unless her condition changed overnight." He made a dismissive gesture with his hand. "I gave her the name. We had to have something to call her."

"Yeah," Ethan said dryly, "guess the name Jane wouldn't work for that."

Knowing the other man could see right through him, Brady tossed up his hands in surrender. "Okay. Okay. So I'm a sucker for a stray. What can I say?"

Ethan settled back in his chair and Brady could feel the full weight of the other man's attention.

"Like I said, there's no law against you taking Lass or Jane or whatever the hell she's calling herself, home with you," the sheriff said, "but you could be asking for a whole heap of trouble. This thing with her smells fishy to me. And the stink could rub off on you or your family. Are you prepared for that?"

Unease prickled down Brady's backbone. He'd been a law officer long enough to know that Ethan was right. Lass could mean trouble. Yet his job was to serve and protect. And right now he couldn't think of anyone who needed his services more than Lass.

"All the more reason to have her in a safe, secluded place. Where I can keep watch on her."

Ethan studied him for long, thoughtful moments, then shook his head. "All right, Brady. I'm not going to buck you on this. Just remember not to let your personal feelings get in the way of the case."

Brady grinned with relief. "I'm not going to stop until

I solve it. In fact, that's why I'm here so early this morning. I was trying to go through the system, see if she might match any new missing person's case."

"What about her fingerprints? Have you already run them?"

Nodding, Brady said, "Did that yesterday. No match there. But then she would've had to have been in the military, the government or arrested to find them in our database."

"What about medical progress?" Ethan asked. "Hank tells me that your sister has taken her case. What is Bridget's medical opinion?"

"That time will heal her. But she can only guess as to how much time."

"Hmm. Let's hope her recovery is speedy. In the meantime, the woman has to be connected to someone. Boyfriend. Husband. Family. Someone who cares enough to start a search for her."

Someone who cares. Ethan's words jerked Brady back to the everyday reality of his job. Of course there were people out there who cared about Lass, he thought. A woman who looked like her most likely had a special man in her life. And it was Brady's job to see that she got safely back to that man's arms.

Chapter Four

Shortly after lunch that same day, Lass's paper work for her release from the hospital was completed and Brady picked her up in a black pickup truck with a sheriff's department seal emblazoned on the doors.

The day was warm and bright and as he drove slowly along a mountain highway, Lass felt her spirits lift. It felt wonderful to be out of the confines of the hospital and even more wonderful to know that she wasn't going to be deposited in a charity ward, where she'd be pushed aside and her plight ignored for those persons with more serious problems.

Turning her gaze away from the passenger window, she glanced over to the man behind the wheel. Brady Donovan was not just a regular deputy, she decided. He was a tall, sexy angel who had rescued her from possible death. If she'd lain on the side of the road throughout the night, she could have succumbed to exposure to the elements or wild animals, particularly black bears. Now he'd come to her rescue again and she wasn't quite sure why.

"You're sure that your family won't mind me staying at their home for a few days?" she asked.

"It's my home, too," he reminded her. "And stop worrying. I spoke to my parents this morning. They're glad to help."

Lass sighed. Most of last night and this morning, as she'd struggled to remember anything about her life up until a day ago, she'd felt totally disconnected, as though she'd been defeated by something or someone, even before she'd received the whack on her head.

"They must be very generous people to allow a stranger into their home." Bending her head, she squeezed her eyes shut as tears threatened to fall. "It would be impossible to express my gratitude to them—to you."

"Forget it, Lass. My family has plenty to give. And they like helping others. They're that sort of people."

Raising her head, she glanced his way. Now in the bright light of day, she was getting an even clearer image of the man and she had to admit that the sight of him was a bit breathtaking. Did that mean that she'd not been accustomed to having a sexy man like him for company? If her memory were working normally, would he still look just as special? Something told her that he would and that she'd never encountered a man like him before.

His tawny-colored hair was shaggier than she'd first noticed and subtly streaked with shades of amber, copper and gold, a perfect foil for his dark green eyes. But the rich colors were only a part of what made his looks so striking, she realized. It was his bigger-than-life presence, the personality that simmered behind his twinkling gaze and enigmatic smile.

"Well, I won't forget this kindness you and your family are showing me. I'll repay you somehow. I promise."

A corner of his mouth lifted in a wry grin. "We don't expect that, Lass. Giving doesn't mean much if you give only to get something in return. That's what my mom always taught me."

Her heart heavy, she gazed out at the desert mountains. They were dotted with twisted juniper, scrubby pinyon pine and clumps of sage. To her right, at the bottom of the mountains, the highway shared part of the valley floor with a river. The Hondo, Brady had called it earlier, was lined with tall poplars, willows and evergreens, while in between the meandering ribbon of water and the roadway, green meadows were covered with grasses and wildflowers. Pretty as the scenery was, nothing about it seemed familiar to her fuddled brain.

"I wonder if I have a mother," she murmured. "I wonder what mine might have taught me."

He was silent for a moment and then the two-way radio on the dashboard began to crackle yet again as a busy dispatcher issued information to an officer on call. By the time the female voice had finished, Lass figured Brady's thoughts had moved on to things other than her miserable plight.

He surprised her by picking up the conversation exactly where Lass had left off. "You're a young woman, Lass. I'm betting you have a mother somewhere. She's probably hunting for you right this moment, and so is…your father."

Lass's heart winced with a doubt she couldn't understand. Why did she have this notion that her parents might not be hunting for her? Wasn't that what normal parents did when their child went missing? Only if they were normal, she mentally pointed out, and God only knew if hers were alive, much less normal.

"I can only hope," she replied, then forcing her mind to move on, she asked, "Does this area have a name? I've noticed we've passed a few homesteads."

"It's called the Hondo Valley. People around here raise cattle and horses and lots of fruit in the summer. Does that ring a bell?"

She bit back a sigh. "Not really."

"Well, if you're not from around here, it probably wouldn't. And I'm positive you don't live anywhere close."

"How could you know that?"

His chuckle was warm and husky and filled Lass with unexpected pleasure.

" 'Cause I know all the pretty women in Lincoln County. And believe me when I say I would know your name."

Forty minutes from the time they drove away from Sierra General, Brady steered the truck off the highway and onto a graveled dirt road lined with a white board fence and towering Lombardy poplars. Along the way, the land opened up to wide meadows with tall dense grass.

When Lass spotted the first mares and foals grazing along the roadside, she squealed with delight.

"Oh! How perfectly lovely!" Leaning forward, she gazed raptly at the horses and, as she took in their grace and beauty, emotion suddenly overwhelmed her to the point that she had to swallow before she could say another word. "Could we…stop for just a minute, Brady? For a closer look?"

"Sure. We're not in a hurry."

He pulled the truck to the side of the road and after carefully helping her to the ground, wrapped his hand firmly around hers, then led her to a spot where the fence was shaded by one of the poplars.

"This is part of the Diamond D's brood stock," he explained as they looked out over the meadow dotted with mares and babies at their sides. "And I'll admit without a speck of modesty that we have some of the finest horses in the southwest."

"Mmm. I wouldn't argue with that," she said as she deliberately fixed her gaze on the horses and tried to ignore the fact that he was still hanging on to her hand. But that was impossible to do when the tangle of their fingers was sending all sorts of hot currents pulsing through her, sensations that she was certain she'd never felt before. Something this strong couldn't be forgotten, she decided.

"You must like horses," he observed. "Maybe you have one of your own somewhere."

She could feel his glance sliding over her and like a magnet it drew her eyes back to his rugged face. Drawing in a deep breath, she replied, "It doesn't make sense but I know…without even thinking about it, that I love these beautiful animals. Strange, isn't it?" she murmured with despair. "I don't know if I have a job, or home or…anything. Yet I feel this affinity to horses."

"We're going to find answers for you, Lass. I promise. And Brady Donovan never makes a promise he can't keep."

Glancing up at him, she gave him a shaky smile and tried not to notice the gentle gleam in his green eyes. As far as she was concerned, Brady Donovan didn't need to carry a firearm. His smile was lethal enough to stop a woman dead in her tracks.

Her heart kicked into a faint flutter, making her words little more than a husky whisper when she said, "I'm going to hold you to that, Deputy."

Carefully extricating her hand from his, she moved a

step forward and leaned against the white fence. The afternoon was warm and a southwesterly breeze ruffled her black hair against her shoulders. The wind carried the scent of pine and juniper and though pleasant, the smells seemed unusual to her. But not nearly so much as the strong reaction she was having to Brady Donovan.

"It's very beautiful here," she went on nervously. "Have you always lived here in this valley?"

"Always," he answered. "All of us six children were born here. My paternal grandparents came from Ireland and settled for a while in Kentucky. That's where my father was born before they moved out here and built the ranch in 1968."

"Are your grandparents still living?"

"My grandmother Kate lives with us. She's eighty-four now and still going strong. My grandfather Arthur died of a stroke nine years ago. He was quite a bit older than Kate. And mean as hell when his temper was riled. But he was a wonderful man."

It was easy to pick up the fondness in Brady Donovan's voice and Lass didn't have to ask whether he was close to his family. Obviously they were a close-knit bunch. And that notion could only make her wonder about herself. Did she have sisters, brothers or both? Was she carrying a family in her heart? One her mind had forgotten?

She was straining to remember the slightest image from her past when a bay mare and brown colt ambled near. Gripping the top rail of the fence, Lass was once again struck with an overload of emotions.

"Oh, what a perfect little filly! She's all brown. Not a speck of white on her!"

Brady smiled fondly at the curious filly drawing near to them. "My sister Dallas calls her Brownie. Of course, that's not her real name. Dad makes sure all of the horses' names go back to their dams and sires. But we usually give them nicknames."

Brownie stuck her nose toward Lass's hand and as she touched the filly's velvety nose, tears blurred her eyes, then fell like watery diamonds onto her cheeks.

Seeing them, Brady softly exclaimed, "Why, Lass! You're crying!"

Instantly, her face blushing with embarrassment, Lass dashed away the emotional tears. "I'm okay," she said with a sniff. "Just feeling a bit...sentimental."

Bending her head, she wiped at the moisture that continued in spite of her effort to gather herself together. Oh, God, what was wrong with her? she wondered. Why would a brown filly with big, sweet eyes reduce her to tears? She was losing it!

Without warning, his arm came around her shoulder and its steadying strength allowed her to lift her head and look at him. The concern on his face touched her, made her long to lay her cheek upon his broad chest and weep until she was too weak to be frightened by the past or worried about the future.

"Have you remembered something, Lass? Is it something about the horses?"

With a brief shake of her head, she forced herself to turn her gaze back on the filly. At the most, the baby horse was probably six months old and would no doubt be weaned in the near future. Her body was long, her tall legs gangly. She was bred for speed and in a couple of years those legs would stretch into a gallop so fast they would appear as little more than a blur.

How did she instinctively know all these things? How did she know about a horse's conformation? Without even thinking she could point out the animal's cannon bone, or hock or withers or any other body part.

"I…don't know, Brady. Something about the horses… When I look at them—especially this brown filly—I feel happy and sad all at the same time. It doesn't make sense. But somehow I'm certain that I know how to ride and ride well."

"Well, that's good news," he said with gentle humor. "That means you're going to fit right in with my family. And while you're here on the ranch you can ride to your heart's content."

She nodded and he squeezed her shoulders.

"We'd better get on to the house," he suggested. "I don't want you to overdo on your first day out of the hospital."

Embarrassed that she'd gotten so inexplicably weepy, she straightened her spine and gave him a grateful, albeit wobbly, smile.

"Thank you, Brady, for stopping and letting me have a few minutes with the horses," she said softly. "And for… everything you're doing for me."

Without warning, his hand lifted to her face and her heart jumped into a rapid thud as his forefinger slowly, gently traced the line of her cheekbone.

"I don't want you to keep thanking me, Lass. I have my own selfish reasons for giving you a temporary home."

Instead of the wild race it had been on, her heart geared itself to a near stop.

"Oh." She unconsciously moistened her lips. "Um…what reasons are you talking about? Making your job easier?"

A lopsided smile twisted his lips. "My job actually has little to do with inviting you to the Diamond D. I like your company. It's that plain and simple. And I guess you could call me a naughty boy for taking advantage of your home-less situation."

She'd not expected anything like this to come from the deputy's mouth and for a moment she was too stunned to make any sort of reply. "Well," she finally whispered, then cleared her throat and tried again, "I have to admire your honesty."

Chuckling lowly, he squeezed her shoulder. "Sorry, Lass. I'm not very good at being subtle, I guess. But don't worry, I promise not to take any more advantages. Unless you…invite me to," he added with a sinful little grin.

Feeling flattered and naive all at once, she drew in a deep breath. "Brady, I—"

Keep everything light, Lass. This lawman is just enjoying a little flirtation with you. That's all.

After her long pause, he prompted, "You what?"

Plastering a playful smile on her face, she said, "I was just going to say that you probably won't enjoy my company for long. Without a memory, I'm pretty boring."

His eyes softened. Or did she just imagine the elusive change in the green depths?

"Let me be the judge of that," he said, then before she could possibly decide how to respond, he turned her toward the waiting truck. "Right now, we'd better get back on the road."

They traveled two more miles before Brady finally stopped the truck in front of a massive two-story house built of native rock and trimmed with rough cedar. Arched windows adorned the front and overlooked a deep green lawn shaded by tall pines.

A brick walkway led to a small portico covering the front entrance. At the double wooden doors fitted with brass, Brady didn't bother knocking. He opened one and gestured for her to precede him over the threshold and into a long foyer filled with potted plants and lined with a selection of wooden, straight-backed chairs.

Instantly Lass caught the scent of lemon wax and the distant sound of piano music.

"That's Grandma Kate pounding the ivories," Brady informed her as they stepped into a long, formal living room.

As they walked forward, Lass caught glimpses of antique furniture covered in rich colored brocade, elaborate window coverings and expensive paintings. The room looked stiff and lonely.

"Is your family musical?" she asked, while trying not to feel conspicuous in her mussed shirt and blue jeans.

Lass would've liked to have purchased something clean to change into before she left the town of Ruidoso, but without money or credit cards, she was hardly in a position to buy anything. And she would have bitten off her tongue before she would've asked Brady for financial aid. He was already bending over backward to help her.

In a flirtatious way, he'd called it taking advantage, but now that she'd had a couple of miles and a few minutes to think about it, she realized he'd only been trying to make her feel as though she wasn't going to be a burden on him, or anyone. There hadn't been anything personal about the look in his eyes or the way he'd touched her. He probably treated all women in that same familiar way and the best thing she could do was put the moment out of her mind.

"Only Grandma and my sister Dallas are the musical ones in the family. I can't tell one note from the other," he answered. With his hand at her back, he guided her through an arched opening and into a long hallway. "The family room is right down here. That's where everybody relaxes and gets together when they're not working. There and the kitchen. Forget the front parlor. That's only used for meeting with people we don't like."

Lass couldn't help but laugh. "Then I'm glad your family didn't meet me there."

After walking several feet down the carpeted corridor, Brady ushered her through an open doorway to their right. The family room, as he'd called it, was a long space, comfortably furnished with two couches and several armchairs, a large television set and stereo equipment, one whole wall of books and wide paned windows that overlooked a ridge of desert mountains. At the far end, a tall woman with graying chestnut hair sat playing an upright piano. The instrument looked as though it had to be near a hundred years old, but the woman pressing the keys appeared surprisingly vital for her age.

At the moment she was playing a boisterous waltz that went a long way in lifting Lass's drooping spirits.

"Grandma! Stop that confounded noise and come meet Lass!" Brady yelled loud enough to be heard above the piano.

Abruptly, the woman lifted her fingers from the keys and turned with a frown. "What? Oh, Brady, it's you."

She rose spryly from the piano stool and walked over to greet them, while Lass studied Brady's grandmother with a bit of shock. She'd been expecting a frail woman with white hair and pale, fragile skin dressed in a flowered shirt-waister. Kate Donovan was a tanned, robust woman, with a short, sporty hairdo and heavy silver jewelry adorning her ears and neck. She was wearing Levi's, cowboy boots and a generous smile on her face. Lass instantly loved her.

"Yes, it's me." He reached out and fondly pinched the woman's cheek and she immediately swatted at his hand.

"Stop it! You big flirt!"

Brady grinned. "That's because you're looking so pretty today."

The older woman feigned a bored sigh, then thrust her hand out to Lass.

"I'm Kate Donovan," she said warmly. "And you must be the little lost lady that my grandson found on the roadside."

Shaking the woman's firm grip, Lass smiled back at her. "Yes, ma'am. And please call me Lass." She glanced shyly toward Brady, then back to the matriarch of the Donovan family. "That's what Brady named me. And I'd like to say how very grateful I am to your grandson—to you and your whole family for allowing me to stay here in your home for a few days."

Kate patted the back of Lass's hand. "You're perfectly welcome, honey. We like having company. When an outsider is around, it keeps the family fights down to a minimum," she added with a wink.

"Grandma, don't make her any more nervous than she already is!" Brady scolded his grandmother. "You'll have her thinking we're a bunch of heathens."

"Nonsense!" Kate shot back at him. "She's probably used to family bickering."

Brady tossed his grandmother a look of exaggerated patience. "Grandma, Lass can't remember anything. She doesn't know whether she has a family, much less if they argue among themselves."

Kate scowled at him. "All right, all right. I wasn't thinking," she admitted. "But it looks as though you don't have an iota of sense in that brain of yours, either."

Confusion caused him to arch one of his brows. "Why do you say that?"

Frowning at him, Kate moved to Lass's side and curled a protective arm around her shoulder. "What do you mean letting the girl leave the hospital in dirty clothes? Shame on you, Brady!"

Brady opened his mouth to speak, but the older woman didn't allow him the chance.

"Don't bother with excuses," Kate said, then turned Lass and began leading her out of the room.

Brady followed on their heels. "What are you doing?"

"Taking Lass upstairs," the older woman answered. "Fiona is already up there, making sure everything is ready for our guest. We'll find Lass some clothes and get her all settled. You don't have to concern yourself now."

"But I—"

Kate Donovan paused in her forward movement long enough to shoot Brady a pointed frown.

"Don't you need to get back to work?" she interjected.

He looked helplessly at Lass, who was still standing beneath his grandmother's protective wing, then shrugged. In all honesty, he wasn't yet ready to leave the ranch and Lass behind. He'd been planning on taking a few more minutes to show her around the house, introduce her to his mother and generally make her feel welcome.

"Ethan lets me be my own boss."

"Poor man," Kate said. "You've got him confused."

Brady hurried over to join the two women as they headed out of the room and quickly looped his arm through Lass's.

"Confused, hell," Brady retorted, then directed his next question at his grandmother. "Have you heard that Penny's pregnant again?"

The older woman paused long enough to gape at him. "Penny? Pregnant again? Why, no! But how wonderful!"

"I'd think shocking is a better word for it," Brady replied. "She's got to be pushing forty."

Kate Donovan laughed and winked at Lass. "Maybe there's still hope for me yet."

"Grandma! Why don't you quit embarrassing me? Old

people should be seen and not heard and you're quickly falling into that category," Brady chided the woman.

Lass gasped while Kate's robust laughter rang through the hallway. "Why don't you move out, big boy?" she suggested to Brady. "And then this house might not feel so much like a mental ward."

Chuckling, Brady bent his head toward Lass's ear. "Grandma and I love each other," he explained. "Very much."

By now the three of them had reached a wide, carpeted staircase, but before they started the climb, Kate stopped and leveled a stern look at Lass.

"Honey, I'm going to warn you right now. Whatever you do, don't believe a word this young fool tells you. He's full of Irish blarney. Or full of himself. Either one is bad for a pretty girl like you."

Before Brady could defend himself, the cell phone in his pocket rang. After one swift glance at the number, he answered, listened briefly, then briskly replied, "Take Tate with you. I expect they'll be some resistance. Yeah. Thirty minutes."

Snapping the phone shut, he dropped the phone in his pocket. "Gotta go," he explained to the two women. "Trouble in the Valley of Fire."

Picking up the urgency in his voice, Lass watched him turn and trot off in the direction from which they'd just came. And as she watched him go, she was suddenly reminded that for all his playfulness, Brady was a lawman and his job no doubt often put him in danger. The idea left her very uneasy.

Kate Donovan patted her shoulder. "Don't worry, Lass. My grandson is a fine deputy. He knows what he's doing."

Yes, but did Lass know what she was doing? She'd come here to the Diamond D to stay until she could figure out where she really belonged. So why did one touch, one smile, from Brady Donovan make her feel like she'd just found home?

Chapter Five

Much later that evening, as night fell over the Diamond D, Lass sat quietly in an armchair in her bedroom. As she watched stars emerge in a purple sky, and wondered how she'd gone from lying unconscious in a mountainside ditch to a luxurious ranch, a light knock sounded on the door.

Maybe Brady had finally returned home, she thought hopefully. All afternoon she'd been thinking about him, imagining him in all sorts of dangerous, life-threatening situations.

Glancing over her shoulder, she called, "Come in."

Instead of Brady pushing through the door, a tall, young woman with light auburn hair and a cheery smile stepped into the room. A crinkled floral skirt swirled against her brown cowboy boots while a coral-colored blouse flattered her vibrant hair. To Lass she looked like a beautiful ray of sunshine.

"Hi," she said. "I'm Dallas. Brady's and Bridget's sister."

Smiling, Lass quickly rose from the chair and walked over to the other woman. Extending her hand, she said, "I'm very happy to meet you, Dallas. I'm…well, I'm Lass." Her short laugh was a mixture of helplessness and humor. "At least, that's what Brady has christened me."

Dallas laughed along with her and Lass instantly realized she was going to like this woman.

"Well, that's much better than the name he gave one of our barn cats. I won't repeat that one to you." She glanced appreciatively over the pale blue dress Lass was wearing. "Hey, that looks great on you. Grandma said that she and Mom found you some of Bridget's things to wear. Since the two of you are both petite and about the same size. But listen, if you'd like to go on a shopping trip, just let me know. We'll take an afternoon and raid all the shops in Ruidoso. My treat. After all, a girl needs intimate things of her own."

"Oh, I couldn't. I mean, Brady didn't find a pocketbook, money, credit cards or anything on me. I'm a—" She held up her palms in a helpless gesture. "I suppose I'm what you call a charity case."

The tall redhead shrugged one slender shoulder. "So what? You won't always be dependant. Besides, I just might put you to work," she added with a wink, then touched Lass's shoulder and urged her toward the door. "If you're ready, let's go down. Dinner is close to being served and the family is having drinks."

Lass followed her out of the bedroom and as they descended the steps, she couldn't stop herself from asking, "Has Brady made it home yet?"

Dallas shook her head. "No. None of us have had any contact with him. One of the hands down at the barns heard over the police scanner that shots had been fired, but that was more than an hour ago."

A heavy weight sunk to the pit of Lass's stomach. "That…sounds ominous."

"Well, Brady has worked as a law officer for a long time and it's pretty rare for shots to be fired. But we try to take it all in stride. He knows what he's doing. And he doesn't want us sitting around worrying about him. But it's definitely hard not to worry. Especially when he was shot last year during a drug sting."

Lass felt chilled. "Shot? Was he wounded badly?"

"A flesh wound in his arm. We were all thankful it wasn't worse."

Hoping the other woman couldn't see the fear in her eyes, Lass murmured, "I'm sure."

The two women descended the last few stairs, then made their way to the family room where Fiona pressed a glass of port into Lass's hand. While she sipped the sweet wine, the woman introduced Lass to Brady's father, Doyle, and his two brothers, Conall and Liam. Surprisingly, the three men were nothing like Brady. Conall was dark and quiet, Liam polite, but with an air of indifference, while Doyle appeared to be a blunt, no-nonsense sort of man.

When the family finally gathered around a long dining table, Lass couldn't help but notice the empty chair to Fiona's left elbow was conspicuously empty. And as the conversation flowed back and forth between the family members, she got the feeling that they were all concerned for his safety, but doing their best to make light of the situation.

"It's probably a drug bust," Fiona said as salads were served by one of the housemaids. "What else would anyone being doing out in the Valley of Fire? There's nothing there but miles and miles of lava beds."

Liam said, "The way Reese heard it over the scanner, the call had something to do with a domestic dispute."

"Way out there?" Dallas countered. "That doesn't make sense. There aren't any homes out there."

Liam frowned impatiently at her. "I'm just repeating what I heard, sis."

"It doesn't matter what the call was about," Doyle said brusquely. "Brady's simply doing his job. He'll be fine. Now let's talk about something else."

At the opposite end of the table from Doyle, Kate cleared her voice loudly. "You're right, son. We have a guest and I'm fairly certain she'd like to talk about something else besides shootings and criminals."

Lass looked up from her salad to find several pairs of eyes on her. Feeling more than conspicuous, warm color flushed her cheeks.

"Oh, please, don't let me interrupt," she said in a small voice. "I'm very happy to just listen."

The older brother—Conall—looked straight at her. Lass got the impression he'd been carved from a chunk of ice.

"So you don't know where you come from?" he asked. "No clues at all?"

"Well, hell no," Kate boomed back at her eldest grandson. "If she did, do you think she'd be wasting her time sitting here, listening to you?"

"I don't know, Grandmother," he said with exaggerated patience. "Maybe she doesn't like where she came from."

Her lips pressed into a grim line, Kate shook her head at him. "Sometimes you can really disappoint me."

He shrugged. "Sorry. I guess I was just made that way," he quipped.

Feeling worse than uncomfortable and wishing Brady was at her side for more than one reason, she tried not to squirm on her seat. She hated to think that some of this family thought she might be faking her amnesia, or that perhaps she might be part of a con, directed at the Donovan family. Didn't they realize that it was all Brady's idea to bring her here? As far as she was concerned, things would have been much simpler if she'd gone to the women's shelter in Ruidoso rather than try to integrate herself into this large, complex family.

"Actually," she said in a low, but steady voice, "I don't know where I used to live. But I believe Brady when he says he'll find my family."

To her surprise, it was Doyle who looked at her with empathy and understanding. "I believe him, too. And until he does, we want you to make our home your home, Lass."

Gratitude poured through her and she smiled briefly at him. "Thank you, Mr. Donovan. I'm very grateful."

Dallas quickly interjected. "Well, I'm happy to learn that Lass remembers something about herself. She knows all about horses and knows how to ride."

Liam's brows lifted with faint curiosity while Conall muttered, "How convenient."

"That's right," Dallas went on, clearly ignoring her brother's sarcasm. "I'm going to take her over to the stables tomorrow and show her around. I think I might have found a great assistant. That is, after she gets over her concussion."

Over a small glass of wine before dinner, Lass had learned that Dallas operated a therapeutic riding stable for handicapped children. Angel Wing Stables, as Dallas had called it, was entirely nonprofit and considered a labor of love. If Lass could help out around the stables in some way, she'd be glad to. She needed something to keep her mind occupied as it tried to heal. And she loved children.

How do you know that about yourself, Lass? Do you have a child of your own? Were you a nurse? A teacher? A mother?

The voice in her head was like tormenting drips of a leaky faucet. The questions were endless and unstoppable.

"By the time she gets over her concussion," Liam reasoned, "she'll probably have her memory back."

"Let's pray that happens," Kate said, then leveled sharp eyes on her grandsons. "You two tough guys over there would be as scared as hell if you woke up some morning and didn't have any roots, or home, or family or a dime in your pocket. Think about it."

They must have thought about it, Lass decided. Because after that, the subject of her amnesia wasn't brought into the conversation again. Talk around the table turned to racing and the fact that Del Mar would be opening for the late summer season soon. In a couple of days, Liam planned to ship several horses out to the historic track in Southern California and would be staying with them until the meet was over in September.

From what she could gather, the Donovans owned several grade I and II thoroughbreds, which was impressive indeed. Horses of that caliber were worth at least a million dollars each and oftentimes more. Which explained the comfortable, but elaborate, house and grounds, the large diamonds on Kate's and Fiona's hands, their casual, but well-tailored clothes. And yet, none of this awed Lass nor made her feel out of place. What did it all mean? That she was also from a rich background? Lass certainly didn't feel rich. But perhaps her inner self wasn't measuring her wealth by money. Thank God.

Not long after the meal, Lass excused herself and climbed the stairs to her bedroom. Brady still hadn't come home and after a few minutes, she climbed into bed thinking about the deputy and listening for the sound of his footsteps on the bedroom landing.

You're clearly unstable, Lass. You don't know your name, where your home is, or if you have one relative on the face of this earth. But instead of worrying about that, all you can think about is a sexy deputy with a head full of tawny waves and hazel green eyes glinting with mischief.

Eventually the nagging voice in her head quieted and Lass fell asleep from the exhaustion of the past two days. She must have slept soundly because the next morning she didn't hear a thing until Brady's voice sounded just above her ear.

"Wake up, sleeping beauty. Coffee has arrived."

The fog of sleep was slow to move from Lass's brain, but when it did, the realization that Brady was standing over her bed and that she was wearing a skimpy gown had her eyes flying open and her hands quickly snatching the cover up to her chin.

"Brady! What…are you doing in here?"

Grinning as though he was pleased with himself, he gestured toward the nightstand and a tray holding a small insulated coffeepot, a fragile china cup and saucer, cream pitcher, sugar bowl and a small branch covered with red blossoms.

"What is that?" she asked.

"Coffee. I took it for granted that you liked it. But if you'd rather have tea, I'll have Reggie prepare another tray."

With a death grip on the sheet, she propped herself against the headboard. A dose of caffeine to wake her up was hardly needed, she thought, when just looking at him was already making her heart pound. "No. I love coffee. I was talking about the flower."

"Oh. That." He picked up the branch of blossoms and handed it to her. "I don't know what it is. I broke it off one of the bushes in Grandma's flower garden. Because it was pretty. And I thought you might like it."

Lass lifted the flowers to her nose, while an awkward feeling suddenly assaulted her. She didn't know why having Brady see her in bed was bothering her. It wasn't like it was the first time. But that had been a narrow hospital bed and she'd been garbed in a thick, unflattering cotton gown. Now she was in an opulent bed wearing a piece of red silk that revealed every curve of her body. And he was giving her flowers as though she was special.

Keeping her eyes carefully on the red, trumpet-shaped blooms, she said, "I do like it. Very much. But Kate's going to get you for meddling with her flowers."

He chuckled. "She'll forgive me. Especially if I tell her I did it for you. She likes you. I can tell. And Grandma doesn't just take to any and everyone."

Turning away from her, he poured the cup full of coffee. "Cream? Sugar?"

It felt ridiculous having this macho man of a lawman standing beside her bed, serving her as though she was a princess. Yet it also made her feel cared about and very special. Was that his motive? she wondered. Or was he this way with all the females who visited the Diamond D?

"Just a little cream, please. But I can do it," she insisted. "You don't need to do...all of this for me."

"Why not? I'm here and I'm capable."

Thrusting her disheveled hair from her face, she placed the flower on her lap and took the cup he offered. While she sipped, he pulled the chair away from the vanity, positioned it next to the bed and took a seat. This morning he was dressed in faded jeans and a black, short-sleeved polo shirt and though his hair was combed neatly back from his face, she could see a hint of rusty whiskers shadowing his chin and jaw. That and the faint lines beneath his eyes were the only signs that he'd had a late night.

"Tell me, Brady, do you do this for all house guests that come to the Diamond D?" she asked as she peered demurely at him over the rim of her cup.

He grinned. "Only the ones I want to leave a lasting impression on," he teased, then his expression sobered. "You have a concussion. You need to be taking it easy."

Unconsciously, her fingertips fluttered to the stitched wound hidden by her hair. "Bridget says I can move around. As long as I don't rush or exert myself. And I'm feeling much stronger today."

"That's good. Real good."

He stretched his long legs out in front of him and crossed his ankles as though he was planning to stay there for a while. Apparently it didn't make him the least bit uncomfortable to visit a woman's bedroom. But then a man who looked like him had probably had plenty of practice at it, she thought.

"We…were all worried about you last night," she murmured. "I'm glad to see you made it safely back home."

He simply looked at her, his eyes warm and appreciative. "It was nothing to get worked up about. Just a little scuffle. A man with a gun got upset and went a little off the beam. That's all. He's safe behind bars now. And we're all just fine."

The first few hours after she'd gone to bed, she'd imagined him in all sorts of dangerous situations and she'd been desperately afraid for his safety. Now, she felt foolish for letting her imagination and her feelings get so out of hand. "Does that sort of thing happen often?" she asked.

"No. But neither does finding a pretty girl with amnesia," he answered, a faint grin lifting one corner of his mouth. "The stars must have gone off-kilter this past week. The department's been extra busy."

"Well, I wish the stars would realign themselves," she did her best to joke. "Maybe then I'd get my memory back."

"Still nothing?"

Staring down at her cooling coffee, she said dismally, "No. Apparently nothing up there in my head is regenerating."

"If Brita says it will, then it will. You just need time," he said with encouragement. Pulling his legs toward him, he leaned forward and rested his forearms across his thighs. "Later this morning Hank and I are going to the track and plaster your picture throughout the clubhouse and betting area. It could be that some of the employees will remember seeing you there last Sunday."

Brady was being so kind and positive the least she could do was be hopeful and optimistic, too. But that was rather difficult to do when every path her mind took, it ran into a black wall.

"But how will that help, Brady? More than likely I didn't give my name to anyone."

"Probably not. But just having someone witness seeing you in a certain place is a big start. If we can confirm that you were at the track that will give us a starting place. From there we can try to trace your steps forward and backward."

She gave him the bravest smile she could muster. "Okay. I trust you."

He chuckled. "Really? Then you're the first woman who ever has."

Was he saying she was gullible where he was concerned? It didn't matter. As far as her missing person case was concerned, she had to trust him. As a man, it shouldn't matter. Even if he wasn't involved with one special woman, she was in no position to get her feelings tangled up with him. With her past a blank, her future could be nothing but uncertain.

Not really knowing what to reply to his sardonic remark, she sipped her coffee and waited for him to take the conversation elsewhere.

"So what are you going to do today? Sit in a stuffed armchair and read a book?"

Wondering if he was serious, she glanced at him. "I have amnesia, not paralysis."

A dimple came and went in his cheek. "Well, if reading sounds too boring you can get Grandma to tell you stories about when she and Grandpa first came here. She has some real humdingers."

"I'm sure. She's quite a colorful woman. But I already have something planned. Later this morning Dallas is taking me over to her stables to have a look around."

He groaned. "Listen, Lass, if you let her, Dallas will drive you crazy talking about all her kids and horses and work. If you get tired, don't be afraid to tell her to hush and bring you home."

Home. Funny how he said it that way, she thought. As though this place was her home, too. The idea touched her and yet at the same time it made her feel a bit weepy. Somewhere there had to be walls and floors and rooms that had made up her home. Had anyone lived in it with her? Had she been loved? The way the Donovans loved each other?

"I'm sure Dallas and I will get on just fine," she told him. "I like her very much."

"Well, as much as I like sitting here with you and seeing you in that pretty red thing you're wearing, I've got to head to work." He rose to his feet, but instead of heading toward the door, he picked up the thermos and refilled the china cup she was balancing on her knee.

His remark about her gown had her eyes flying downward and she realized with a start that the sheet had slipped to expose her bodice. Thankfully, the paper-thin silk was still covering her breasts.

With a tiny gasp, she started to reach for the sheet, but realized the movement was causing the coffee to slosh dangerously near the rim of the cup.

"Don't worry about it," he said with a little laugh, then taking pity on her, started toward the door. "You look beautiful. Just the way I imagined you would." With his hand on the knob, he gave her one last glance. "Unless an emergency comes up, I'll see you later this evening. And who knows, by then someone searching for you might contact the sheriff's department."

"I guess that could happen," she said, while wondering why she couldn't muster up more enthusiasm over the idea.

"Sure it could," he said cheerfully. "And then all your problems will be solved."

He gave her a little salute then stepped out the door. Once it clicked behind him, Lass's shoulders sagged against the pillows. Would finding her past really solve all her problems, she wondered.

Somehow she didn't think so. Something kept swirling around in her brain, some dark elusive thought that kept whispering the words *danger* and *fear*.

Later that morning, dressed in her own boots, and the jeans and blouse that the maid had laundered for her, she climbed into a pickup truck with Dallas and the two of them headed south on a graveled road toward a ridge of desert mountains.

"Looks like we're going into the wilderness," Lass commented. "I thought your stable was probably located close to the highway. For convenience."

Smiling, Dallas shook her head. "When I first got the idea to build the stables, I knew I wanted it to be far away from the things that most town kids see every day. Like concrete, asphalt and the whiz of vehicles. I wanted it to be an escape for them." She jerked the steering wheel to avoid a pothole. "I admit that the trip back here isn't like a drive to the country club. But I believe all in all, it's worth it for the children." She glanced at Lass. "I guess this is a silly question, but do you think you have children or a child of your own?"

Sighing, Lass stared out the window at the passing desert landscape. Instinctively, she felt she'd come from a place where huge trees shaded deep green lawns. Yet when she thought of something personal, like a husband or children, her mind revolted and turned as blank as a clean blackboard.

"That's a question I've been asking myself, Dallas. And when I try to remember if I ever held a baby of my own…" She paused and shook her head miserably. "I don't feel as though I've ever had a child. Dear God, I hope there's not a baby out there somewhere crying for me and I have no way of knowing—of getting back to him or her."

Brady's sister nodded grimly. "Yes. I can see where that thought would be torturous."

"Bridget did say that it's unlikely I've given birth. Still, that doesn't mean there isn't a child out there waiting for me."

Three miles from the Diamond D ranch yard, beyond the mountain ridge, two huge barns and several smaller buildings were erected in a meadow not far from a small creek. Dallas wasted no time in taking Lass through the barn where the horses were stalled, the tack and feed kept and the outside riding arena. Because the day was growing very warm, Dallas had decided to move the riders to a smaller, indoor arena where the temperature was regulated.

Whenever they stepped inside, Lass was surprised to see several stable assistants had children already mounted and moving slowly over the carefully raked ground. Some had outward problems that were obvious to any onlooker, like leg braces or a missing limb. Others suffered the less obvious, such as mental and emotional handicaps. But to Lass's delight, they were all smiling and having a good time.

"This is wonderful!" Lass exclaimed as she twisted her head in an effort to take everything in. "The children appear to love it!"

Dallas's eyes twinkled with pride. "They do. And the interaction with the horses helps them in ways you wouldn't believe. I hope while you're here you'll get a chance to see all the positives that go on here," she said.

"I think I'm seeing it right now," Lass told her.

Taking her by the arm as though she'd known her for years, Dallas urged her forward. "C'mon and I'll introduce you to everyone."

Much later, while Dallas went to deal with a few of the more problematic riders, Lass was content to find a seat on a hay bale behind the fenced arena. She was concentrating on the children and watching the interaction between them and Dallas, when a slight movement caught her eye.

Turning her head slightly, Lass saw a tall, dark-haired man tethering a white horse to a hitching post. There was nothing unusual or out of sorts with the man or the animal and she was on the verge of turning her attention back toward the arena when images suddenly began to flash in front of her eyes.

A steel-gray horse wearing a bright red blanket, a saddle being tossed upon its back. A tall, faceless man in tan chinos, his hand gripping her wrist.

You're coming with me. Coming with me. Coming with me.

The male voice chanted the words over and over in her head, wrapping the phrase around the flashing images until everything became a violent blur.

Releasing a faint sob, she dropped her head in her hands and supped in long, cleansing breaths. If she was actually remembering, she didn't want any part of it.

"Lass? Are you okay?"

Dropping her hands away from her face, she looked up to see Brady's sister standing over her. The woman was looking at her with concern and for a moment Lass wondered if she'd unconsciously cried out in fear.

"I...um, my head is starting to pound again. That's all." She didn't want to tell Dallas about her visions just yet. Not until she'd spoken to Brady. He was the one who'd rescued her. He was the one who was working to find her identity. And he was the one she trusted to make some sort of sense of her predicament.

"Oh. I'd better get you back to the house!" With a hand on Lass's arm, she helped her to her feet. "I'm so sorry, Lass. I've probably put too much on you this morning. Brady is going to be furious with me."

"Bridget is my doctor. Not Brady," Lass pointed out.

A knowing smile crossed Dallas's pretty face. "Yes. But my brother considers you his lost and found."

Dallas's words should have lent her some sort of comfort. After all, what normal woman wouldn't want to be tucked under the protective wing of a sexy lawman like Brady?

But Lass wasn't a typical woman. And after experiencing those strange visions a few moments ago, she feared her hopes for a normal future were in jeopardy.

For the remainder of the day, Lass stuck close to the house and generally tried to relax. But that was difficult to do when her head was spinning with the unbidden images she'd experienced at Dallas's riding stables. Everything about them had scared and confused her and she was desperate to see Brady again. Not only to tell him what had happened, but also to see his smile, to hear his strong voice assuring her that everything would be all right.

She was sitting on a covered porch at the back of the house, two of the family's pet cats curled at her feet, when she heard footsteps behind her. Expecting it to be Fiona or Kate inviting her in for drinks, she was more than surprised to see Brady.

"Mom told me where you were," he explained as he approached her chair. "Why are you sitting out here all by yourself?"

Even though he was still in his work clothes, he looked wonderful to her and before she could contain herself, she jumped to her feet and threw herself against his chest.

"Oh, Brady, I'm so glad you're home!" she practically sobbed.

His face a mixture of pleasure and confusion, he wrapped his arms around her and held her close. "Whoa now, Lass, there's not any need for you to be so worked up. I haven't had anybody shooting at me today. That was last night."

Sniffing, she tilted her head back and looked up at him with misty eyes. "I'm sorry for being so…melodramatic, Brady. You must think I've lost my mind. And I—" With an anguished groan, she twisted out of his arms and turned her back to him. "I'm afraid I have. I apologize for throwing myself at you like that."

His low chuckles were suddenly brushing against the back of her neck and suddenly the quivering in the pit of her stomach had nothing to do with fear.

"You think you need to apologize for hugging me? I just wished you'd hung on longer."

His suggestive remark had her swallowing, fighting the urge to turn to him once more. "I don't think…that would be wise," she said, her voice breathy and broken.

"Why?"

She couldn't summon an answer and then it didn't matter as his hand pushed the curtain of her long hair to one side and his lips settled softly on the back of her neck.

"Because I might do this," he whispered against her skin. "Or this?"

With his hands on her shoulders, he turned her toward him and all Lass could do was stand motionless and wait for his kiss.

Chapter Six

Since the night Brady had found her in the ditch and propped her limp body in the circle of his arms, he'd wondered how it would feel to hold this woman in a romantic embrace, imagined how her lips would taste. Yet none of those mental images had come close to the actual thing he was experiencing now.

He knew he should be resisting her. He should remember how vulnerable she was, that she looked to him for protection. But she'd made the first move, and he wasn't the type to refuse a beautiful woman. Especially not this one.

Tucked close against him, her body felt small and soft and incredibly warm, while her lips tasted like sweet fruit. Ripe. Juicy. Delicious. Her hands were planted against his chest and though her fingers were small, they were sending shock waves of heat straight through the fabric of his shirt and onto his skin.

Brady could have stood there kissing her forever if she'd not finally broke the contact of their lips and squirmed her way out of his arms. And even then, as she stood there looking at him with wide, wondrous eyes, he wanted to gather her back against him, to experience the pleasure of her all over again.

"I'm sorry. I…must have sent you the wrong signal," she finally said in a raw whisper.

He couldn't stop a grin from lifting one corner of his mouth. "Which time? When you hugged me? Or when you kissed me?"

Groaning with embarrassment, she covered her mouth with her hand. As though he'd just marked her in some way and she didn't want him or anyone to see the change in her.

"Both times!" she exclaimed, then dropped her hand and stared at him in a beseeching way. "Please forget that. Every bit of it!"

Brady could see she was deadly serious, but still he couldn't prevent the low chuckles that rippled up in his throat. She was just too precious, too beautiful. "Are you kidding? I'm not about to forget something that wonderful."

Her nostrils flared and he watched the rapid rise and fall of her bosom as images of her in bed this morning assaulted his already lust-filled brain. The thin red silk had revealed the exact shape of her nipples, the perfect round curves of her breasts. He'd wanted to touch her then. Just as badly as he wanted to touch her now.

"Brady, I need to explain. I—"

"Lass, there's no need for you to break apart over a little kiss. You're carrying on as though you've never been kissed before," he teased in an effort to ease the moment. Clearly she was distressed and he didn't understand exactly why. He knew enough about women to know when one was enjoying being kissed and Lass had clearly been enjoying it.

She grimaced. "I wouldn't know! I don't remember what I've done in the past! Or who I've done it with," she practically snapped, then shook her head with dismay. "Forgive me, Brady. I…seem to be breaking apart, don't I? And I'm trying so hard to hold myself together. But this morning—"

She trailed off and Brady stepped forward and reached for her hand. To his relief, she wrapped her fingers around his and held on tightly.

"What about this morning?" he urged. "Did something happen while I was gone?"

Sighing, she closed her eyes. "I'm not sure. Maybe I've worked myself up over nothing," she told him. "But whatever I saw in my mind won't go away. That must mean it happened. Wouldn't you think?"

Not fully understanding what she was trying to say, he led her to a wicker love seat shaded by a curtain of morning glory vines.

"Okay, Lass, start over. Are you trying to tell me that you've remembered something?"

She nodded soberly. "I think so. But I'm not sure. I was with Dallas at her stables this morning. Just sitting there watching the children. And then I saw one of the stable helpers tending to a horse and something happened in my head. All of a sudden images were flashing in front of my eyes."

"What sort of images?"

"A steel-gray horse was being saddled by someone. I don't know who. The blanket was bright red and the saddle was the English sort. Then the horse was suddenly gone and a man was standing in front of me. He was gripping my wrist. Really hard. And he kept saying over and over, 'You're coming with me.'"

Everything inside Brady went still. "Did you recognize this man?"

"No. It was like a dream where you never see the face. It was someone tall with dark hair."

"What about the voice? Did you recognize it?"

Shaking her head, she said, "It seemed familiar, but I can't identify it. To be honest, the voice scares me, Brady. I—" She gripped his hand even tighter. "All day it's been haunting me. Now, after desperately wishing I could remember something, I'm wishing I could forget this."

Placing his free hand on top of hers, he said, "I wouldn't put much stock into the whole thing, Lass. Whatever you saw could be something that happened years ago. Or maybe you had a dream last night and it suddenly came to you."

She didn't look at all convinced and to be honest Brady found it hard to dismiss her images as dreams. From the small amount of time he'd been around this woman, she didn't appear to be an airhead or a drama queen. True, she was a bit upset at the moment, but anyone in her predicament had a right to feel unsettled.

"I don't think so, Brady. I think those were glimmers of things that happened—before I was injured."

"Could be, Lass. But we won't know for certain until you have more of them, or I manage to get a toehold on some relevant information. And I hate to tell you, but that hasn't happened yet. No one at the track seemed to recognize you. A waitress in the club house restaurant thought she recalled seeing you, but she wasn't sure. When they see hundreds of faces a day, it's hard to single out one from the crowd."

"Oh, well," she said, trying to put a bit of cheer in her voice, "someone might eventually see my picture and identify me. I mean, I couldn't have come from Mars. Martians don't wear cowboy boots and Levi's, do they?"

Glad that she could see a bit of humor in the whole thing, he smiled, then leaned forward and pressed a light kiss against her forehead.

Behind them, a door opened, and Kate made a production of clearing her throat. "The family is having drinks. Are you two going to join us?" she asked.

Knowing this intimate time with Lass was over, at least, for now, Brady rose from the love seat and reached for Lass's hand.

"Grandma, did anyone ever tell you that your timing is rotten?"

Kate grinned. "Looks to me like my timing was perfect. I saved Lass from your clutches."

Easing his arm around Lass's waist, he urged her toward Kate and a door that would take them back into the house. "What's wrong with my clutches?" he asked his grandmother. "Lass just might like them."

With a good-natured snort, Kate turned and entered the door before them. "She's too smart a girl for that, sonny."

Lass was quickly learning that dinner at the Donovans' was a special affair. Tonight, Opal, the family's longtime cook, had prepared prime rib, and as each course was served, the conversation seemed to change to a different subject. By the time dishes of strawberry torte arrived for dessert, Conall was giving a production report of a gold mine that belonged to their sister, Maura. Since the elder brother was manager of the Golden Spur's operations and part of the profit was distributed to the whole family, it was a subject that held everyone's attention.

Except Brady, it seemed. He seemed more interested in Lass than anything and each time he turned his twinkling eyes on her, her mind insisted on replaying the kiss he'd given her on the back porch.

What had prompted him to do such a thing? But then what had been behind her behavior? The moment he'd walked onto the porch, she'd thrown herself at him like some sort of starved lover. Was that the way she normally acted around attractive men? Before she'd lost her memory had she been promiscuous?

No, Lass refused to believe that. Deep down, she felt certain it wasn't her nature to casually jump into a sexual relationship with a man. She hadn't felt anything for Hank, or the doctors or even Conall. So she couldn't exactly understand what had come over her with Brady. Except that all day long she'd been desperate to see him, talk with him. She'd certainly not had kissing the man on her mind. She'd been all wound up about those memory flashes and then when he'd finally shown up, relief and joy had shot her straight to his arms, nothing more. Now he was looking at her as though she was part of the dessert. And all she could think about was the magic she'd felt when his lips had touched hers, the way his hands had caressed and pulled her close.

For the remainder of the meal, she tried to push the whole incident out of her mind and by the time everyone finished dessert, she'd convinced herself that she was being silly to dwell on one little kiss. Brady hadn't taken it seriously and neither should she.

As everyone filed out of the dining room, Brady excused himself to make an important phone call. Since it was still too early to retire to her room, Lass followed Kate and Brady's parents to the family room.

While Kate played a medley of Irish folk songs on the piano and Fiona and Doyle started up a card game, Lass picked up a newspaper and began to scan the headlines.

She was reading about a government proposal to bring aid to drought-stricken ranchers, when Brady eased a hip onto the arm of her chair.

"Catching up on the news?" he asked.

She glanced at him, while wishing her heart wouldn't jump into high gear every time the man drew within ten feet of her. "Trying," she admitted, then gave him an encouraging smile. "You know, when I started reading the headlines, I realized that I remembered who our president is and most of our national officials. Strange, that I can remember something like that, but not my own parents."

His brows peaked with interest, and he gestured toward the paper. "Were there any stories in there that sparked your memory? A town? A name?"

"Not really. But that's not surprising. I'm obviously not a local." A thoughtful frown puckered her forehead. "When I look at some of the addresses listed on these advertisements, I keep thinking I should see a TX rather than NM."

"So you're thinking you might be from Texas?"

Nodding stiffly, she said, "I'm hardly certain of that. It's just a gut feeling." As she looked at him her eyes suddenly widened. "Brady, maybe I had a rental car! You could trace it! Or perhaps I flew in from Texas to the Ruidoso airport? Will they have records?"

"I've questioned the staff at the airport. None of them recalled seeing you. As for passenger records, the personnel at the airport has promised to go through them, but since we don't have your name, it's impossible to know when you arrived, or even if you arrived by plane. So that effort might not lead to any sort of productive information. Hank has already checked all the car rental places in town. Nothing there. So that means you probably took a taxi. We've left your photo with all the cab services. But I'm not expecting much to evolve there. There are simply too many tourists and strange faces in town and a cabbie would've only seen you for few short minutes at the most. Plus there's still the possibility that someone else drove you to the track."

"Someone else drove me to the track," she repeated blankly. "Like who? If I was with a friend or relative where are they now? Why did they leave me on that mountain road?"

"I understand that possibility doesn't make sense to you, Lass. But as a lawman, I have to go at things from every angle. Some person you met in town could have simply offered you a ride to the track out of kindness, then left town after the races."

"I see," she murmured, while wondering why this news left her feeling so confused. She wanted Brady to discover her real identity, didn't she? Of course, she did. Her whole life was missing. And yet, a part of her didn't want to return to who she'd been before. A part of her wanted to start her life right here. Right now. With him. Oh, God, what was happening to her?

"Come on, you've worried about all that stuff enough for one day. Do you feel like a walk?"

Grateful that he understood she needed a break from the turmoil going round in her head, she smiled at him. "I'd love to take a walk."

He helped her from the chair, then ushered her out of the room before his parents or grandmother even noticed they were leaving. At the end of a long hallway, near a door composed of paned windows, he snatched a white shawl from a rack on the wall.

"You might get a little cool," he explained as he draped the crocheted lace around her shoulders. "Mom won't mind if you borrow her shawl."

Swallowing nervously, she focused on the front of his pale yellow shirt instead of his face. "Thank you, Brady."

"My pleasure."

When they stepped outside, Lass could see they were at the side of the house. It was shaded deeply by tall ponderosa pines, but footlights illuminated a graveled path leading to the front and back of the huge rock structure.

"Let's go to the backyard," he suggested as he splayed a hand against her back. "Have you been down to the pool yet?"

"No. I've only gotten as far as the porch," she admitted.

He ushered her forward and they began to slowly walk abreast. He'd been right about the air turning cool. The temperature felt as though it had dropped several degrees, but the touch of his hand felt so hot against her, it chased any chilliness away.

Breathing deeply, she tried not to think of his nearness or the way it had felt to kiss him.

"Do you like living here with the rest of your family?" she asked as they strolled along a walkway of loose river gravel.

"I can't imagine living anywhere else." He darted a glance at her. "That probably sounds like I lack ambition, doesn't it? You're probably wondering why a man like me doesn't want a place of his own."

"I'm not wondering anything like that," she admitted. "I see a man who loves his family."

"Hmm. That's true. But I don't hang around here because I'm too green to cut the apron strings."

Lass smiled in the darkness. Green was the exact opposite of the image he portrayed, she thought. He was strong, brave and independent. The exact opposite of... whom? For a split second, a man's image almost popped into her head, but it was so fleeting and her mind so weary, she didn't bother to try to catch it.

"I would never think that," she assured him.

His hand moved downward until his fingers were curled snugly around the side of her waist. "You're being very polite."

"I'm not just being polite. I'm being honest."

He chuckled then. "Well, I guess to the outward person my brothers and I look like mama's boys. But that's not the case at all. Conall and Liam run the ranch operations. Without all their work, Dad wouldn't be able to retire and enjoy these years with Mom. And me, well, I don't do ranch work on a day-to-day basis, but I help as much as I can."

"That's something I've been curious about," Lass told him. "Why did you become a lawman? Particularly, when your brothers are ranchers like your father."

They walked for several yards before he finally answered and by then they'd entered a garden filled with ornamental bushes and low, blooming flowers. The graveled path had turned to stepping stones and the sweet smell of honeysuckle filled the night air.

Brady paused to face her. "I'm lucky, Lass. From the time we were young children, our father has always encouraged us to follow our own dreams. If that meant something other than raising thoroughbreds, then that was okay with him."

"You don't like working with horses?"

There was a perplexed frown on her face, as though she couldn't imagine anyone opposing such a job. It made Brady realize just how much she loved horses and that she'd no doubt been involved in the equine business in some form or fashion. But that was a wide-ranging possibility that included farms, ranches, tracks, trainers, stables and veterinarians, coupled with all the offshoot jobs from those businesses. Unless she remembered something helpful, finding her identity was going to be like searching for one tiny mosquito in the middle of a giant swamp.

Keeping that worrisome thought to himself, he said, "Oh, sure. I love horses. But I never had that special touch with them. Not the way my father and brothers have always had. They understand what a horse is thinking and planning way before the horse even knows it. And I…well, I learned the hard way. By being bit or kicked or bucked off. You get the picture. But that didn't matter. I just happened to have other ideas about my career. And it wasn't breeding or racing horses."

She nodded that she understood his independence wasn't born out of retaliation. "How did you decide you wanted to be a lawman? You have other relatives in the business?"

He chuckled. "I wish. Then everyone wouldn't look at me like I'm the lone wolf of the bunch." Curling his arm around her shoulder, he once again urged her forward. "Actually, I first planned to be a lawyer. A horse farm of this size always needs legal work and I liked the idea of laying out rules and regulations."

"A lawyer," she repeated with faint amazement. "I can't imagine you in a courtroom."

"No? Well, Grandma could imagine me in that role. She said I could argue better than anyone she knew," he teased. "But after I started college it didn't take me very long to realize I didn't want to be confined behind four walls for the rest of my life."

"So you quit college and went to work for the sheriff's department?"

"Not exactly," he answered. "I went to work part-time for the sheriff's department, did my rookie training and continued earning a degree in criminal justice during my off hours. All of it together was tough going for a while.

But now I'm glad I put out the effort." With a wry smile, he glanced down at her. "I took the long way about answering a simple question, didn't I? So I've talked enough about myself. Let's talk about you."

By now they had reached a long, oval-shaped pool surrounded by footlights. The crystal clear water sparkled invitingly and as she stared at the depths, she envisioned herself in a similar pool, the water slipping cool against her arms, the night air above her hot and humid. She tried to hang on to the image, to memorize every detail, but like before, it was gone almost as quickly as it came and with a frustrated sigh, she said, "We can't talk about me, Brady. I don't know anything about me."

Seeing the whole thing disturbed her, Brady urged her over to a flowered lounge positioned a few feet from the edge of the pool. After she took a seat on the end of the long chair, he sank next to her and reached for her hand.

"I'm sorry, Lass. I wasn't thinking. Damn it, I've never been around anyone who can't remember who they are and I keep forgetting to watch my words. Everything I say seems to put a glaring light on your predicament."

Shaking her head, she stared pensively into the darkness. "That's all right. I don't want you to watch your words around me, Brady. I want you to be yourself. I don't want you to try to isolate or cushion me from reality. I'm tougher than you think. Really I am."

Brady couldn't stop his hands from wrapping around her slender shoulders or turning her toward him. There was something sweetly endearing about her that pulled at everything inside of him. Something about the trusting look in her gray eyes that made him want to be her protector, her hero, her everything.

"Tough is not the way I'd describe you, Lass," he said

lowly. The holes in the crocheted shawl exposed patches of skin to his hands. The soft feel of it excited him, almost as much as gazing at the moist curves of her lips. "Strong. But not tough."

Her lashes fluttered demurely against her cheeks. "Brady, we came out here for a walk," she pointed out. "In case you hadn't noticed, we're sitting."

He rubbed the top of his forefinger beneath her chin and swallowed as the urge to kiss her threatened to overtake his senses.

He murmured, "As a deputy of this county, I can assure you that sitting isn't a crime."

The tip of her tongue slipped out to nervously moisten her top lip. "Brady, that kiss…earlier—"

"Yes?"

"I don't think we should repeat it."

She looked confused and worried and for the first time in his life, Brady felt a bit of unease himself. Which didn't make any sense. Kissing a beautiful woman had never concerned him before. He didn't know why it should give him second thoughts now. But kissing Lass had been different, he realized. So different that he wanted to do it over. He wanted to make sure it had actually felt that amazing.

"Why?"

Her mouth fell open. "You have to ask? Brady, I can't even tell you my name! I don't even know how old I am!"

He cupped his palm against the side of her face as his thoughts rolled back to the night he'd found her lying lifelessly in the ditch. When she'd finally regained consciousness and he'd sheltered her in his arms, he'd experienced some very unprofessional feelings and since he'd gotten to know her, those unprofessional feelings had only deepened. Hell, that was enough to scare any tried and true bachelor. But it didn't scare him enough to make him rise to his feet and walk away from her.

"Of course you can tell me your name," he insisted. "It's Lass."

"Only temporarily."

Ignoring that, he said, "And you certainly look old enough to kiss."

She sighed. "Kate says you're somewhat of a ladies' man."

He grimaced. "Grandma has a motormouth."

"Then she was speaking the truth?"

Since she wasn't trying to pull away, Brady made the most of the close proximity by delving his fingers into her silky hair, sliding them downward through the long strands.

"Look, Lass, I'm not going to pretend I've been some sort of saint. Especially when—"

"When I can't even tell you what I've been," she finished miserably. Then biting her bottom lip, she looked away. "I'm sorry, Brady. I had no right to question you about your past. Not when mine is a complete blank."

"Lass, Lass," he softly scolded, "no one has to give me your résumé for me to know that you are and were a lady. And in spite of what Grandma says about me, I'm a gentleman."

Her eyes softened and then to Brady's amazement, her face drew near to his. "Yes, I think you are," she whispered.

The moment their lips touched, Brady realized he'd made a mistake. Her kiss didn't just taste amazing; the sensations went far deeper than that. Like tremors of an earthquake, waves of pleasure vibrated through him, urged him to crush her close, to search out the mysterious sweetness of her lips.

Seconds could have passed or minutes, he didn't know, but suddenly he felt her arms go around his neck and the sign of surrender brought a groan of triumph deep in his throat. Her lips parted wider and he took advantage, slipping his tongue past their sweet curves and into the honeyed cavity of her mouth.

The intimate connection caused his head to reel and before he could get a grip on his senses, their surroundings began to float away. His hands began to urgently roam her body, his lips fought to totally capture hers and in the process he forgot everything but making love to the woman in his arms.

Until her hands slipped to his shoulders and pushed, her lips abruptly jerked away from his.

The sudden break jolted him and as he attempted to gather himself together, he wanted to ask her what was wrong, why had she interrupted something so incredible.

But one look at her face answered those questions for him. The two of them had been on the verge of losing control, of making love right here beside the pool. And she wasn't all that happy about it.

Pushing a tangle of hair from her eyes, she said in a husky voice, "I think we've 'walked' enough for one night. Don't you?"

Did she really expect him to answer that? He looked away from her and drew in several long, mind-cleansing breaths. What was happening here? He wasn't supposed to want Lass this much. He wasn't supposed to want any woman this much.

Rising from the chair, he reached for her hand. "You're right, Lass. We'd better go in. Before our walk turns into a run."

Chapter Seven

He'd been wrong to kiss Lass.

The next morning, as Brady drove south to the Mescalero Apache Indian Reservation, that dismal thought continued to swirl through his head. He'd misjudged the whole thing and instead of it being a pleasant little connection of the lips, the kiss had turned out to be a heated embrace that had turned him on his ear and left her strangely quiet for the remainder of the evening.

Now, all he could do was relive the experience over and over in his mind and wonder what it all meant. That the two of them had great chemistry together? There was no doubt about that. But he'd dated attractive women before and some of those occasions had turned into overnight delights. Yet he could easily admit that nothing about those unions had messed with his thinking or left him in such a mental fog. Lass was doing something to him. Something that he didn't understand or want to acknowledge.

Sighing, he glanced over to the empty seat of the pickup truck outfitted with a two-way radio, weapons and other police equipment. This morning he'd left Hank back in Ruidoso, scouring the more popular restaurants and motels where Lass might be remembered by the staff.

Normally, a case like hers wouldn't receive this much investigative work from the sheriff's department. Instead, Lass's case would have fallen under the health and welfare services. But thankfully Sheriff Hamilton had agreed with Brady that the circumstances surrounding Lass's amnesia smelled of criminal mischief and needed to be resolved.

Brady had no idea how long Ethan would keep the case open or how much time and manpower he would expend toward it. With county cost a factor, Brady knew the search couldn't last forever. He couldn't imagine having to tell Lass the effort to find her home and family had to come to an end. In fact, if it came down to it, Brady would use his own resources to find Lass's identity.

But he prayed to God before any of that happened, something would turn up. Or even better, Lass would start to remember. Until then, Brady had his work cut out for him. Not only to find Lass's past, but to also keep his growing attraction for the woman in a proper perspective. And his hands to himself.

Yeah, right, he thought, as he turned down the bumpy dirt road to the Chino homestead. That was like telling himself to quit eating whenever he was hungry.

Johnny Chino was two years older than Brady and had lived with his grandparents, Charlie and Naomi, since he was a tiny infant. His mother had been an unwed teenager, a wild and irresponsible girl who'd been spoiled since her parents were older when she was born. She'd brought much shame on the Chino family. Shortly after Johnny had been born, she'd dumped the baby into her parents' lap and left for parts unknown. A few years later, they'd gotten word that she'd been killed in an alcohol-related car crash.

Now Johnny's grandparents were both in their nineties, but were still in good enough health to do for themselves. Even so, Johnny didn't stray far from the home place and Brady often wondered if they were the reason the man had quit taking on tracking jobs. Rumor had it that he'd quit because of some tragedy that had occurred out in California. But Brady wasn't one to listen to rumors. Nor was he one to question a friend just to satisfy a curiosity.

When Brady parked the truck in front of the house, two dogs, a red hound and a black collie, barked and ran toward the vehicle. Trusting that the dogs would remember him from his last visit a couple of months ago, he stepped to the ground.

By the time the dogs had surrounded him, a door slammed and he looked up to see Johnny stepping onto the long, wooden porch spanning the front of the small stucco house.

He was a tall, strongly built man, his long black hair pulled into a ponytail. His right cheekbone carried a faint scar, but it was his dark eyes that bore the true marks of his past. He stood where he was and waited for Brady to join him in the shade.

Lifting his hand in greeting, Brady approached the porch. Their tails wagging, the dogs trailed close on his heels.

"They remember you," Johnny said, nodding toward the dogs.

"Why wouldn't they?" Brady joked. "I'm pretty unforgettable."

A quirk of a smile moved a corner of Johnny's mouth as he motioned to a tattered lawn chair. "Come sit."

Brady climbed the steps and took a seat. Johnny slouched against the wall of the house and pulled a piece of willow from his pocket and opened his pocket knife.

"How are your grandparents, Johnny?" he asked politely.

"Old. Very old."

Well, his friend always did have a way of summing up a situation with very few words, Brady thought wryly.

"You probably know why I'm here," Brady said. In spite of this part of the reservation being remote, he knew that news of any sort traveled quickly from one family to the next. No doubt Johnny had already heard a woman had been found in the mountains.

"Maybe."

Brady did his best to contain a sigh of impatience. This was one man he couldn't hurry and if he tried, he'd probably blow the whole reason for the visit.

"The girl doesn't know who she is," Brady explained. "And I can't figure out what happened. At least, I haven't yet."

"I'm no lawman."

"No. But you'd make a good one," Brady said honestly.

Johnny's knife blade sliced through the piece of willow and a curl of wood fell to the porch floor.

"I don't track anymore."

Brady couldn't let things die there. Lass and her happiness meant too much to him. "I was hoping you'd break out of retirement for me. Just this one time."

"The dogs don't track anymore, either."

Brady looked around to see both dogs had flopped down in a hole they had scratched near the end of the porch. Their energy level appeared to match Johnny's.

"Since when have you needed dogs to help you?" Brady asked.

"I don't track anymore," he repeated.

Rubbing his hands over his knees, Brady tried to hide his frustration. "Johnny, I thought we were friends. Good friends."

Johnny's rough features tightened, but he said nothing.

One minute, then two, then three finally ticked by in pregnant silence. If it had been anyone else besides Johnny, Brady would have set in with a long speech about how they'd stood up for each other in high school, how they'd always had each other's backs on the football field, and how after Brady's grandfather had died, they'd camped together on Bonito Lake for a whole week. Because at that time, Johnny had understood how much Brady had needed to be with a friend.

But Brady didn't remind the other man of their close ties. He knew that Johnny hadn't forgotten anything.

"This girl," Johnny said finally, "she means a lot to you?"

Brady let out a long breath. Means a lot? Leave it to his old buddy's simple question to make Brady really think about what Lass was becoming to him, how important her happiness had come to mean to him. "Yeah. She…well, I like her better than any girl I can ever remember."

His friend didn't make an immediate reply to that and while Brady waited, he watched a pair of guinea hens strut across the dusty yard. He tried to imagine Johnny living in Albuquerque or Santa Fe, but that was like picturing a mountain lion in a cage.

"Show me where you found her," Johnny finally said. "And I'll try to get the dogs interested."

More grateful than he ever expected to feel, Brady swallowed a sigh of relief, then rose to his feet and walked over to Johnny.

At that moment, he could have said a lot of things to his old friend. Like how much he valued their friendship. How much he appreciated his help and how much he thanked him for always being around whenever he needed him. But Johnny already knew all of that. And the quiet Apache would be insulted to hear such platitudes from Brady. To Johnny a true bond needed no words to keep it strong.

Instead, Brady touched a hand to his shoulder. "Fine. But before we go, I'd like to say hello to your grandparents."

Johnny opened the front door of the little stucco and motioned for Brady to precede him into the house. As Brady stepped into the cool, dimly lit living room, all he could think about was that he was now one giant step closer to finding Lass's identity.

But what was that going to bring to her? To him? Was all of this effort to find her past, eventually going to tear her from his arms?

Brady couldn't let himself think about those questions. Because the minute he did he would quit being the Chief Deputy of Lincoln County and simply become a man.

At the same time, some twenty miles away, in a small boutique in downtown Ruidoso, Lass ambled slowly through the aisles of lingerie while close behind her, Dallas made helpful suggestions.

"I love this pink lace," Dallas said, pausing to examine a set of bra and panties draped from a padded satin hanger. "This would look great on you, Lass."

A faint blush colored Lass's face. "Those are very expensive. Especially when…well, no one is going to see what I'm wearing underneath," she reasoned.

"Lass! Since when did a woman start worrying about that? We wear this stuff because it makes us feel sexy and pretty. And who's worrying about the cost, anyway? I'm not."

Following up on her invitation from yesterday, Dallas

had insisted on bringing Lass to town today to shop for personal items. So far she'd purchased a sack full of inexpensive makeup, hair-styling tools, two pair of shoes, a handbag and wallet. Though what she expected to put inside the wallet, she didn't know. Without money, ID, credit cards, or a checkbook, she had little use for one. But Dallas had insisted, saying eventually that Brady was going to solve the whole thing and then Lass would need a place to put her driver's license and other important information.

"I can see that you're not concerned about the expense. But I am," Lass told her.

Dallas rolled her green eyes. "Oh, Lass, I rarely leave the stables to do anything. Much less shopping. And to have someone else to buy for makes this spree all that much better. Now please don't spoil my fun. Come on and loosen up. Pick out your size in this pink and then we'll find something in black. With your hair color you'll sizzle!"

Sizzle? Lass didn't need black lingerie to make her sizzle. Brady could easily get that job done.

Oh, Lord, why couldn't she quit thinking about the man? Why couldn't she get last night out of her mind? she wondered, as a flush of embarrassed heat warmed her cheeks. She'd never behaved so recklessly with a man. Never felt such a raw, unbridled urge to make love.

So how do you know that, Lass? Your mind is a blank blackboard. It can't tell you whether you've had a boyfriend or lover or even a husband! How can it tell you that Brady made you feel things you've never felt before?

Because something deep down, something more than her mind was speaking to her, she mentally flung back at the little voice.

To Dallas she said with a measure of uncertainty, "I'm not really sure I want to sizzle, Dallas."

Dallas laughed. "Honey, every woman from nine to ninety wants to feel a little spark now and then. And even though no one can tell us your exact age, I think we can safely assume you fit somewhere in that category."

With a good-natured groan, Lass followed Dallas's orders and searched through the pink lingerie until she found the correct size. But as the two women moved on down the aisle, past the cotton undergarments, Lass touched her friend's arm.

"Dallas, wait a minute. Look at this stuff. Have you stopped to consider that I might be a cotton sort of girl?"

Dallas shot her a look of wry disbelief and Lass made a helpless gesture with her hands.

"See what I mean! I don't remember anything about myself. It's…scary. I could have been a mousy little librarian afraid to date even a nerd or—God forbid—maybe I was one of those women who flaunted themselves and had boyfriends scattered all over town!"

Dallas began to laugh, then, spotting the distress on Lass's face, she gently curved a reassuring arm around her shoulders.

"I'm sorry, Lass, I know that none of this seems funny to you. But the idea of you being either one of those types of women is ridiculous. You have amnesia, not a personality disorder. Believe me, if Brady had thought you were wild and crazy, he wouldn't have brought you home to the ranch. And trust me, he's a good judge of character."

After last night, there was no telling how he was judging her character, Lass thought. Stifling a groan, she said, "Well, I'm just very grateful that he decided to help me. That all of you are helping me."

Dallas gave her shoulders another squeeze. "Look, Lass, I'm actually a selfish person. I love having your company. Brita's so busy with her career as a doctor and Maura's time is consumed with her own family. She has an eighteen-month-old son, Riley, and two weeks ago she gave birth to another son, Michael, so I don't have a sister to pal with anymore and you're the next best thing. The fact that you're a horsewoman like me just makes it even better." She shook her head with wry disbelief. "Isn't it destiny," she went on, "that you ended up on our horse farm?"

Destiny? Sometimes Lass felt as if she were in the twilight zone or some freakish dream that was too good to be true. She worried that at any moment she would wake and be jerked back to some dark place she didn't want to be.

"Very," Lass agreed. "And if your brother hadn't found me that night—I might not even be alive today."

Dropping her arm from her shoulders, Dallas urged her on down the aisle and away from the cotton underwear. "I can tell my brother likes you," she declared. "A lot."

Lass glanced around the store, as though she suspected anyone hearing such a comment would burst out laughing. From what Kate had told her, Brady's acquaintances with women ranged all over the county and beyond. He'd never lacked female attention. In fact, Kate said that more often than not, Brady had more trouble getting rid of a girlfriend than acquiring one. And after that kiss he'd given Lass last night, she could certainly understand why. The man's charm was so strong it deserved a warning label.

Picking up a black camisole, she studied the lace edging that would frame her bosom in a very provocative way. "I understand that Brady likes *a lot* of women," Lass murmured as she fingered the whisper light silk.

Dallas grimaced with disapproval. "Yes. But not like this. Not like you."

Lass jerked her gaze to the other woman's face. "Why do you say that?"

"Because he's never brought any woman home to the ranch before. And he darn sure wouldn't let one near Grandma. Not unless he considered her to be *really* special."

Could Dallas be right? Lass wondered. Did he consider her special? As soon as the question crossed her mind, she berated herself for even thinking it. She couldn't allow herself to get all dreamy-eyed about Brady. Any hour, any day, someone could show up to claim her. And then what would happen? Where would she be? What sort of life would that someone lead her back to? No, getting involved with Brady would be the same as asking for a heart ache.

Later that evening, more than thirty miles away at the sheriff's department in Carrizozo, Brady was sitting at his desk, searching through page after page of data on the computer screen, when a cup of steaming hot coffee appeared a few inches from his right hand.

Glancing up, he saw Hank's beaming face.

"What's this for?" Brady asked the junior deputy.

"I just made a new pot and you looked like you needed it."

"Thanks. I do need it. It's been a hell of a day and it's not over yet."

"You're telling me. Ever since I came back from lunch, the darn phone has been ringing off the hook." Hank motioned toward the monitor. "Find anything on there that fits Lass?"

"This is the first chance I've had to look today. And so far I'm not finding any missing persons alerts that even come close to Lass's description." He reached for the foam cup and took a cautious sip while Hank pulled up a folding metal chair and flopped into it.

This afternoon, while Brady had driven Johnny to the mountains, the department had been flooded with an array of calls. For the past several hours, Hank had been out doing his part to deal with the problems. Brady glanced at his watch. It was getting late, but before he left for the ranch, he needed to talk over Johnny's findings with Ethan. But for the past hour Ethan had been tied up with meetings and phone calls. Today had been a busy day for all of them and Brady was feeling more than tired. He was frustrated and troubled and more than a little anxious to see Lass again.

"I'm glad you showed up before I head home," he told Hank. "I need your reports from this morning. Have you had a chance to type them up?"

Hank looked at him with a bemused expression. "Reports? I didn't go out on any calls this morning."

Brady slowly lifted his gray hat from his hand and stabbed his fingers through his flattened hair. "Hank, I sent you out to question the businesses on Sudderth and Mechem Drives. You were supposed to ask if anyone working in those businesses recalled seeing Lass in the days before we found her. Remember?"

"Well, sure I remember what I was doing this morning. I just wasn't considering that the same as going on a call. You sent me on that job. It wasn't the same as somebody calling in and wanting help. Don't you see?"

Brady sighed. "Yeah. I see. So where are your notes? I understand that you've been tied up most of the day, so if you've not had a chance to type them up, we'll worry about that later. Just give me what you have and I'll try to decipher your handwriting."

Hank's expression turned sheepish. "I ain't got no notes. Nobody knew nothin'. So there wasn't any use in taking down notes."

Screwing his hat back onto his head, Brady narrowed his eyes on the hapless deputy. Hank was usually a dedicated deputy. And ever since he'd been hired on at the department, he'd been a good friend to Brady. But at this moment he wanted to wring the man's neck.

"No use, huh? I don't know what makes me angrier at you, Hank. Not following orders or using double negatives!"

His face red, Hank cringed back in his seat. "Brady, that's not fair! I talked to a bunch of people. Waitresses and clerks and cleaning people. You name it and I talked to 'em. They all looked at Lass's photo and none of them remembered her."

Frustration boiled over and Brady's hand slapped down so hard on his desk that the coffee came dangerously close to slopping over the rim and spilling onto the ink blotter.

"Since when did Sheriff Hamilton decide to change department policy around here?" Brady boomed at him. "Maybe we should call him out here and ask him? He might need to know that you've taken it upon yourself to decide what information is worthy of being noted or ignored."

"No! Oh, hell, Brady, please don't tell him about this!" Hank pleaded, then suddenly his expression turned hopeful and he dug into the front pocket of his jeans until he pulled out a small scrap of paper. Tossing it onto Brady's desk he added, "I almost forgot. That's for you."

With a cursory glance at the paper, Brady asked, "What is it?"

"A telephone number. From that little redhead at the desk at the Aspen Hotel. She asked me to give it to you."

His back teeth grinding together, Brady wadded the paper into a tight ball and threw it at the junior deputy. "I'm not interested in some little redhead!" He regained control, stabbing a finger toward the outer office. "Go type up your work, and if nobody knew anything, then put it down that way! And I expect you to list each business you walked into and each person you said one word to. Got it?"

Hank jumped up from the chair so fast that it tipped over and clattered loudly to the hard tiled floor. Before Brady could say more, he scrambled to right the chair, then scurried from the room as though a bolt of lightning was nipping at his rear.

On the opposite side of the room, the door to the sheriff's office opened and Ethan's face appeared around the edge of the wooden panel. "What in heck is going on out here?"

Brady wearily wiped a hand over his face. "Sorry for the interruption, Ethan. Hank knocked a chair over."

Sensing that Brady was dealing with more than a tumbled chair, Ethan stepped into the room.

"I heard yelling. That's not like you, Brady."

Brady grimaced. It was rare that he raised his voice to anyone. But this whole thing about Lass, about what Johnny had discovered about the night she was injured, was tearing at him. "No. Hank set me off and I...lost my cool with him."

Ethan took a seat in the chair that Hank had vacated only seconds ago. "Well, Hank can be a handful to deal with. But he means well. What has he done now?"

Sighing ruefully, Brady rubbed the tight muscles at the back of his neck. In spite of his frustration, there was no way he wanted to get his partner in trouble. "Nothing that bad. He...just needed a reminder to follow orders. That's all."

Accepting his explanation without further question, Ethan glanced thoughtfully at the computer screen, then back to Brady. "Any leads about Lass?"

"Only what Johnny found."

Ethan arched a quizzical brow at him. "You got Johnny Chino to venture off the res for Lass's case?"

There had been a time when the department had relied on Johnny's tracking skills to help them solve cases or find lost children. But that had ended long ago when Johnny had abruptly called it quits. No doubt the sheriff was surprised to hear the man had emerged from the reservation to offer his help.

"We were in the mountains all afternoon."

"And?"

Brady fought the urge to bend his head and close his eyes. This was business, not personal, and he needed to treat it as such. Yet the whole idea that Lass had possibly been running for her life haunted him in ways he'd never expected it to.

"Plenty. He found the spot on the side of the highway where the vehicle she'd been riding in had stopped. A scuffle ensued there and then Lass ran into a nearby ravine. Her attacker—companion, or whatever the person was—followed. But he must have lost Lass in the dark because his tracks climbed back out of the steep crevice and returned to the car. Lass's tracks continued on up the mountain. Johnny found where she'd tripped over a fallen branch and hit her head on a slab of rock. After that, she wandered due west until she reached the road and collapsed in the ditch."

Ethan's thumb and forefinger stroked his chin as he silently digested this new information. "Did Johnny think the car drove up the mountain to look for Lass? After four days the elements have probably erased most of the readable evidence. But that Apache can see things no one else can see."

"Actually, I asked him that same question," Brady told him. "And Johnny believes the car pulled back onto the highway, headed east and never returned. After Lass fell and wandered to the road, no one else's tracks appeared."

"Hmm. So in other words, whoever was driving the car left Lass alone in the mountains. And so far, he hasn't shown his face to us. That tells us plenty."

"Yeah," Brady said grimly, "he was up to no good. And he has no intention of showing up to claim her."

Ethan nodded. "Even if the wound to her head occurred because of the fall, that doesn't clear the jerk from wrongdoing. Clearly he was trying to harm her. But who and why? Has she remembered anything else?"

"Only confusing fragments. I talked to Bridget about it and she seems to think that remembering things, no matter how small, is a hopeful sign. She believes Lass's memory will return sooner than later."

Ethan rose to his feet. "This is not just a case of amnesia, Brady. It's a criminal case, but we pretty much assumed that from the very start. So I don't expect you to sit around and simply wait for Lass to remember who tried to hurt her. Keep doing what you're doing. Searching—for anything and everything."

Brady nodded soberly. "I will."

His expression full of concern, Ethan laid a hand on Brady's shoulder. "So what are you going to tell Lass about this? About Johnny's findings?"

Brady glanced up at him. "I have to tell her everything, don't I? What other choice do I have?"

Ethan released a heavy breath. "None, I suppose. It's her life, she deserves to know what happened." Giving Brady's shoulder another pat, the sheriff gazed pensively off in space. "I'm thinking back to a time before Penny and I were married, when she was still the county judge. A crazy escaped convict was sending in threats to the sheriff's department that he intended to kill her. I had to be the one to tell her that some other human being hated her that much.

Then I had to try to capture him and keep her safe. It wasn't an easy task."

"Was that before you two started a relationship?" Brady asked curiously.

One corner of Ethan's mouth lifted wryly. "That's when I fell in love with her."

Something inside Brady tumbled, then hit with a hard jolt. What was Ethan trying to tell him? That if he didn't watch his step he'd be falling in love with Lass?

His mind was spinning, searching for some sort of sensible reply to the sheriff's remark when Ethan spoke again, thankfully on a different subject.

"So what are you going to do about Hank?" Ethan asked. "We don't want him moping around here like a whipped pup for the rest of the week."

"I'll make it up to him," Brady assured him.

Ethan chuckled. "How do you plan to do that? He's not yet ready for a promotion."

A tired grin crossed Brady's face. "I'll set him up with a blind date. He thinks having a woman in his life will fix everything."

Grunting with amusement, Ethan headed back to his office. "Don't we all?"

Thoughtful now, Brady watched the sheriff close the door behind him. Having Lass in his life for these few days had been nice. No, he corrected, it had been more than nice. The time with her had been special. Really special. But that didn't mean his life before Lass had needed fixing. Did it? That didn't mean he'd become a broken man if she suddenly went back to her old life.

Turning back to the computer screen, Brady muttered a curse under his breath. He was damned stupid for letting Ethan's simple question get to him. After all, he'd always been a strong guy. He'd always been in control of his emotions, his happiness. One pretty little gray-eyed lass wasn't going to change that. Was she?

Chapter Eight

In spite of the heavy workload, Brady managed to make the drive home to the Diamond D and shower before dinnertime. Once he dressed and combed his hair into a semblance of order, he left his room, then stopped at Lass's door on the chance that she'd not yet joined the rest of the family downstairs.

Rapping his knuckles on the wooden panel, he called to her in a low voice, "Lass? Are you in there?"

After a couple of moments he heard her light footsteps and then the door swung wide. Brady's pulse stumbled, then leaped into a fast race as he drank in the sight of her petite figure sheathed in a pale blue dress that fit at her waist and flared at her knees. The neckline was daringly low. At least, in his mind, it dared him to take a second and third look at the tempting hint of cleavage exposed above the fabric.

"Brady," she greeted with faint surprise. "Am I...late for supper or something?"

He smiled gently while he tried not to stare. There was a faint bit of makeup on her face and her black hair was coiled into intricate loops atop her head and fastened with rhinestone pins. She looked so lovely it made him ache in a way he'd never ached before.

"Don't worry. I doubt the family has gathered yet. I...wanted to talk to you before we went downstairs," he told her.

Her gray eyes earnestly searched his face. "Oh. Is anything wrong?"

He said, "Not exactly. May I come in?"

"Of course."

With slightly flustered movements, she pushed the door wider and Brady entered the bedroom. The faint scent of her flowery perfume lingered in the air and from the corner of his eye he could see a few silky undergarments scattered across the end of the queen-size bed. For one reckless moment, Brady easily imagined himself pulling scraps of satin and lace from her slender body, of laying her on the bed and...

Before he could let his mind finish the erotic vision, he grabbed her by the elbow and maneuvered her over to a sliding glass door that opened onto a balcony.

"Let's go out here," he suggested. Where he could get some fresh air and hopefully forget how much he wanted to make love to this woman.

The balcony floor was made of planked timber and spanned the whole width of the house. Furniture made of redwood and covered with cushions of bright floral fabric was grouped along the wide expanse, so that each bedroom was provided with a variety of comfortable seating. Potted bougainvillea, agave and aloe plants were scattered here and there, but it was the huge loblolly pines towering over the front edge of the deck that made the spot feel truly outdoors.

As Brady helped her into one of the chairs, she spoke in an attempt to lighten the moment. "Should I be whispering? We'd have to go down to the barn to get much farther from your family."

Brady eased onto the edge of the chair facing hers and leaned toward her. He'd never brought his work home with him before. And he'd always made a point of never getting personally involved with victims of a crime. A lawman had to work with his head, not his heart. But with Lass he'd broken his own rules.

Now he understood why Ethan had initially discouraged him from bringing Lass into his home. Danger could possibly be following her right here to the Diamond D. Yet he'd known that from the very start. And from the very start, he'd not been able to resist her.

"They'll hear it later. Right now— I wanted to discuss this with you first."

Her gray eyes suddenly filled with uncertain shadows. "You've discovered something. About me. About what happened."

He nodded, then awkwardly broke his gaze from hers to stare over her shoulder at the gathering clouds. Ethan was right again, he thought bleakly. It wasn't easy to tell a person that someone had intentions to harm them. Especially a soft, gentle woman like the one sitting in front of him.

"Yes. This afternoon, my friend—Johnny Chino, an Apache that I grew up with—scouted the area where we found you in the mountains."

She looked completely puzzled. "I don't understand,

Brady. It's been four, nearly five days since the accident. What could this man possibly find after that length of time?"

A corner of his mouth lifted in a wan grin. "You'd be surprised. He can pick up a trail that most normal people would fail to see. And, we've had a bit of luck with very little wind and no rain occurring these past days."

She drew in a bracing breath and Brady couldn't stop himself from reaching for her hand and wrapping his fingers around hers.

"So what did he find? My handbag? Pieces of clothing? More wagering tickets from the track?"

"No. He didn't find items, Lass. He found a story."

Her pink lips parted as she stared at him and Brady fought the urge to pull her out of the chair onto his lap, to kiss her until the lipstick was gone, along with the burning need inside him.

"A story?" she repeated blankly.

Brady nodded. "It has a few holes, but enough of the plot is there to tell us part of what happened that night you lost your memory."

Her free hand crept up to her throat, as though she feared his next words, as though the unconscious part of her mind already knew it was an ugly story. Brady desperately wanted to ease her fears, to assure her that he would always keep her safe. God, what was it about this woman that made him feel so protective? he wondered. Until Lass came along, he'd never wanted to be any woman's knight in shining armor.

"Tell me," she whispered.

As concisely as possible, Brady related the evidence that Johnny had found, including the exact way she'd fallen and struck her head, to the direction she'd been walking when she'd collapsed in the ditch.

When Brady's words finally died away, Lass closed her eyes and tried to digest it all, tried to attach it to the strange images that had continued to flash through her mind at odd moments, but it was all so horrifying, so confusing, she could pull none of it together.

"Oh, God, Brady, someone really did try to harm me!" Her eyes flew open and looked straight into his. "I mean, logically, I knew that I hadn't just wandered off in the mountains on my own. Without any car it was obvious that someone had driven me there. But this—why? Why would I have been struggling with someone?"

Before Brady could answer, she jumped to her feet and walked blindly over to the wooden balustrade surrounding the edge of the balcony. Tears burned her eyes as she stared past the pine boughs, to the distant mountain ridge. At the moment, dark clouds were churning over the tall peaks, while intermittent flashes of lightning warned of oncoming rain. She could only think how the turbulent weather matched the turmoil inside her.

"Lass, I'm sorry," Brady said softly as he walked behind her and wrapped his hands over her shoulders. "I wish… that none of this had happened to you."

A hysterical sob bubbled up in her throat. She not only had amnesia, she thought sickly, but she'd gone crazy along with it. Because a part of her wasn't sorry that someone had nearly killed her. Otherwise, she would have never met Brady. Otherwise, she would have never known his touch, his kiss, the pure joy of being near him.

Twisting around to face him, she said in a stricken voice, "But it has happened, Brady! And where is this person now? What if he's hanging around, waiting to hurt me again?"

With a heavy groan, Brady circled his arms around her and Lass gladly settled her cheek upon his broad chest.

Bending his head, he whispered against the top of her hair, "No one is going to hurt you here on the Diamond D, Lass. You may not realize it, because they're dressed like the rest of the cowboys around here, but we have plenty of security roaming the ranch. Many of our horses are worth six and seven figures each. You don't take chances with them. So if anyone shows up without a reason for being here, the security guys will know it."

"But Dallas and I went shopping in town today!" she exclaimed. "He could have been stalking us. He—"

His arms tightened to pull her even closer. "Is more than likely long gone from this area. And if he isn't, then I'll catch the bastard. In the meantime, I don't want you leaving the ranch alone for any reason. And if you do leave with anyone, I want to know about it first. Okay?"

Lass couldn't stop a sliver of fear from snaking down her spine. "I understand."

His forefinger slid beneath her chin and lifted her face up to his. "You trust me to take care of you, don't you?" he asked softly.

With her safety, yes. Her heart? That was another matter. Yet where this man was concerned, it seemed to ignore the fact that he was a self-admitted bachelor and her future was a big question mark. At this moment, she couldn't stop it from pounding with joy at being in his arms, feeling the warmth of his hard body pressed against hers.

"Yes," she murmured. "I trust you."

The pads of his fingers gently brushed her cheek, then trailed downward along the side of her neck. Without looking up at the sky, Lass sensed that the distant clouds had now moved over them. But to her, the oncoming storm wasn't nearly as dangerous to her well-being as this man she was clinging to.

"I hear a 'but' in your voice, Lass."

She sighed as his hand moved to the skin of her bare back. "That's because I'm afraid I'm beginning to trust you too much, Brady."

"That's impossible," he whispered. "Just like it's impossible for me not to kiss you."

This time Lass didn't hide her desire for him or wait for him to bend his head to hers. Rising up to her tiptoes, she angled her mouth to his, then moaned with satisfaction as he took what she offered.

The tender movement of his lips against hers was the complete opposite of the fiercely heated kiss they'd shared by the pool, yet it was equally potent, touching her senses, her heart so deeply, that her hands clutched him for support, while her body wilted and wallowed in the pleasure he was creating inside her.

Brady's body was burning, his mind threatening to lose all common sense, when suddenly a whoosh of cold wind swept across the balcony and, close on its heels, fat rain drops spattered around them like warning signals from heaven.

Lifting his head, Brady grabbed her hand. "We'd better get inside before we get drenched."

By the time they entered the bedroom and Brady had safely secured the glass door behind them, lightning was cracking ever so close. Thunder rumbled loudly, followed by more wicked flashes of raw electricity.

Clutching her arms to her waist, Lass looked at him and tried to push away her disappointment, to tell herself that it was probably for the best that Mother Nature had decided to interrupt their embrace.

A few steps away, Brady spoke her same thoughts, only for a different reason. "It's probably a good thing the rain ran us inside," he said as he shook a few drops from his hair.

"It's time for dinner and if we don't show up soon, Grandma will come looking for us. She's just like Dad, grumbling and groaning if one of us is late to the dining table."

Lass suspected he was right. The older woman had already come searching for them last night when she and Brady had been kissing on the porch. If Kate had seen then what was going on between her grandson and Lass, she'd never mentioned it. But Lass figured the woman missed nothing that went on in the Donovan house.

After the kiss Brady had just given her, she needed to repair her lipstick, but she wasn't going to waste the time. Instead, she said, "In that case, we'd better hurry. I don't want her upset with me."

Chuckling, he put his hand to the back of her waist and ushered her out of the bedroom.

As they quickly crossed the landing, Lass said in a thoughtful voice, "I wonder if I had a grandmother like Kate."

"Let's hope not," he teased.

Lass cast him a hopeless look. "What am I doing wondering about grandparents, anyway? I'm a woman who doesn't even know if she has parents!"

"Of course you do. Someone gave birth to you, raised you."

"Then why aren't they looking for me?"

As she and Brady reached the stairs, he paused to look at her. "Your parents could be looking for you, Lass. Just not in the right place yet."

Regret clouded her eyes. "When you tell Fiona and Doyle about…what happened to me on the mountain, they're not going to be pleased. They might even want me to leave before trouble follows me here to the ranch. And I probably should."

His hands were suddenly gripping her upper arms. "Not

in a million years, Lass! My parents already understood there was a possibility you'd met with foul play. They'll be concerned, but they'll hardly be afraid or want you to leave. They've dealt with trouble before. And they have six children of their own. They'd want someone to shelter and care for one of us if we were in your predicament."

Sighing, she pressed fingers to the tiny ache in her forehead. Since she and Brady had ran in from the rain, her head felt odd and it was a struggle for her to keep her thoughts focused on anything. What was the matter with her?

"Well, I can only hope that my parents come close to being as kind and generous as yours."

With a confident grin, he tucked his arm through hers and guided her down the long staircase. "They'd have to be, Lass, to have a daughter as lovely as you."

His compliment put a wan smile on her face and as they continued on down the stairs, she tried to put the troubling thoughts out of her head, but the more she tried to push them aside, the more her mind began to jump erratically from the story that Johnny Chino had revealed, to the faceless man gripping her arm, gritting out a menacing order to follow him.

"Oh!" Without warning, everything began to swirl wildly around Lass. She swayed drunkenly and grasped blindly for the staircase railing.

"Lass!" With his arm planted firmly around her waist, Brady steadied her on her feet and helped her off the last stair. "What is it?"

Squeezing her eyes shut, she pressed a palm to her forehead. Her breaths were coming short and fast and a fine layer of sweat now covered her face.

"I—I don't know. I…" The rest of her words trailed away as behind her closed eyes, the vision of a woman's face suddenly appeared. She had graceful features and coal-black hair, but it was her soft smile that pierced Lass right in the middle of her chest. That gentle, understanding smile was the same one that had soothed Lass down through the years, had encouraged her to face her fears and always put forth her best effort.

Mother? Yes. Her dear, sweet mother.

Bending her head, Lass fought to hold on to the image, to connect it to a name, a place. And then without warning, Lass could see herself standing next to a grave. The mound of dirt was covered with fresh flowers and a crowd of mourners was gathered in the quiet cemetery. She sensed that her father was at her side, but she couldn't look at him. Couldn't bear to hear him say that her mother was truly gone.

"Oh, God. Oh, no!" With a sob catching in her throat, Lass lifted her head to stare at Brady. Sorrow, dark and heavy, fell over her, while angry fists pounded at her heart. "I—I've remembered my mother," she finally managed to say in a broken voice. "And—she's dead, Brady. I don't have a mother anymore."

Clearly stunned, Brady studied her wounded face. "Lass," he began softly, "are you certain about this? Maybe you're seeing some other relative, or a friend?"

"No. It's my mother. My heart is telling me it's my mother. I can't give you her name or where we lived, but I do know that the image was her and that she…is gone."

As she spoke the last word tears welled in her eyes and spilled onto her cheeks. Brady gathered her into his arms and cradled her head against his chest.

"It'll be okay, sweetheart. I promise."

He was stroking her back, waiting for her sobs to subside, when footsteps sounded on the hardwood floor and he looked around to see his grandmother approaching them. No doubt she and his father had grown tired of waiting and Kate had come to let the hammer down.

But after one sweeping glance of the situation, Kate's annoyed expression turned to concern. "What's happened?"

Brady was shocked to find he had to swallow before he could answer his grandmother's question. "Lass has remembered her mother."

Kate arched a brow at him. "That's good, isn't it?"

Over Lass's head, Brady exchanged a troubled look with his grandmother. "It would be—but she's remembered that her mother has passed away."

"Oh, the poor little darling." Immediately, Kate marched forward and gently eased Lass out of Brady's arms. "Come on, honey," she said to Lass, "let me take you to the family room where you can lie down."

As Brady watched his grandmother slowly lead Lass away, he felt oddly empty and more than shaken. To see Lass in such grief had been the same as someone stabbing him with a knife. And the moment Kate had pulled Lass from his arms, he'd wanted to snatch her back.

He was the one who should be consoling Lass. He was the one who wanted to soothe her tears, make her happy. But how could he ever expect to do that? He couldn't even give her something as simple as her real name.

Chapter Nine

For the next week and a half Lass tried to come to terms with her mother's death and the reality that something unhappy had been going on in her former life. Along with reflections of her mother and the menacing man gripping her wrist, snippets of another person had been entering her mind at unexpected moments. Even though names and places still eluded her, Lass was quite certain the image was that of her father—although she'd not yet gotten a clear picture of his face, she recognized his big frame and deep voice.

Each time her father's image flashed through her mind, she was consumed with sadness and confusion. Clearly, all had not been right between father and daughter. But Lass had no idea what had brought about such dissension in the family. She only knew that whatever had occurred now left her feeling cold and empty.

Bridget had continued to check on Lass every day and

the family practitioner kept insisting that Lass needed to start talks with a mental therapist. But so far Lass was reluctant to begin. She'd already remembered enough to tell her that she'd left bad things behind her. Why should she let a therapist, or anyone for that matter, send her back to that place? Lass didn't want to go back. She wanted to move forward. And perhaps that was the crux of the matter, she thought dismally. Like the psychiatrist in the hospital had initially suggested, her mind refused to remember, because she simply didn't want it to.

Still, Lass was smart enough to understand that she couldn't live in limbo forever. The time would soon come when she would be forced to seek help from a medical specialist. But in the meantime, she wanted to live as though she was as normal as the next person.

These past days, Lass had worked at Dallas's riding clinic from early in the mornings to late in the evenings. She'd been doing everything from grooming and tacking the horses to assisting the children with their rides.

The task of dealing with both children and horses couldn't have been more perfect for Lass. The job had given her more than pleasure; it had filled her with new confidence. Now she felt as though she was serving a useful purpose rather than sponging off the Donovans. And the fact that Brady had been showing up at the stables these past few evenings made the job doubly pleasurable.

Dallas had told her that occasionally in the past, whenever his work schedule allowed, Brady showed up at the stables to donate his time and labor to whatever was needed around the place. But she insisted that her brother had never appeared at the stables for several days running. Usually his social calendar took up most of his free time.

Dallas attributed his sudden interest in the stables to

Lass's presence, but Lass wasn't convinced that was the only reason Brady had been spending time at the riding clinic. He seemed to genuinely care for the children and went out of his way to make them happy. On one particular evening, he'd ridden for nearly an hour behind the saddle of one very small girl just to help her gain confidence in handling her mount. And last night after everyone had dismounted and gone into the barn for refreshments, he'd gathered the children together and told them a funny story that had kept them all laughing.

Seeing Brady at the stables had shown Lass a side of him that she'd never expected to see. In spite of his single-guy image, he dealt with the children as any good father would. And even though he'd told Lass that he didn't have a special touch with horses, he handled and rode them better than she and Dallas put together.

Lass was learning there were many more sides to the man and each one he revealed drew her to him even more. Yet she continued to remind herself that her time with Brady was borrowed. Where he was concerned, she couldn't give her emotions free reins. Not if she ever expected to leave this ranch with her heart fully intact.

They had not kissed again, though Lass hadn't been able to forget that last kiss. An occasional holding of hands and a few touches and gentle kisses had been all the contact they'd had. And Lass had tried to convince herself that it was what she'd wanted.

Even so, this particular evening, she'd found herself glancing around, wondering if or when he was going to show up. After a very busy day, things were beginning to wind down and now only a handful of children were mounted and circling their horses around the outdoor arena.

Earlier this afternoon, Dallas had gone to Ruidoso for

business reasons and left Lass in charge of operations. So far Lass hadn't run into any problems. Except for one little boy with dark brown hair, a metal brace on his leg and a very sad look on his face. His name was Tyler and since his arrival a couple of hours ago, he'd never left his seat on the bale of hay stacked near the arena fence. Earlier Lass had tried to coax him into the saddle, but he'd refused to budge.

Now, with plans to try again, she walked up to the boy. "Tyler, aren't you getting tired of sitting there? Would you like to walk with me over to the saddling corral?"

"Nope. I like it here," he said stubbornly.

"Oh. Well, I think it's time I rested my feet. Do you mind sharing your seat?"

He shrugged one slender shoulder. "Suit yourself."

After easing down beside the child, Lass crossed her boots out in front of her. "Is this your first visit to the stables?"

Looking bored now, the boy shook his head. "Nope. I was here once before—a long time ago."

"Hmm. I guess that was before I started helping around here," she said thoughtfully. "Did you ride a horse then?"

"Nope. I didn't want to ride then and I don't want to ride now," he said flatly. "The only reason I'm here is because my mom made me come."

"Awww," Lass groaned with disappointment. "That's too bad. When I first saw you sitting here, I thought to myself, now I'll bet that young man loves horses almost as much as I do. I guess I was really wrong about you."

His lips clamped into a tight purse, but it was simply taking more strength than he could muster to hold them that way for long. Suddenly words began to burst from him like air from a balloon.

"That ain't so! I love horses!"

Lass smiled to herself. "Really? That's great to hear. So why aren't you riding today?"

He pulled a face at her that said she must be blind or stupid, or both. "Can't you see? I gotta wear this brace. I can't bend my leg."

Lass had already talked to Dallas about Tyler's condition and she'd learned that eventually the brace would be removed and the boy's leg would be straight and perfect enough to walk, run and jump like any normal child. But in the meantime, Tyler clearly thought that day was a lifetime away.

"So? That doesn't mean you can't sit in the saddle. You're sitting on this hay bale, aren't you? And Ms. Dallas has already saddled Cloudwalker for you. He's a pretty black-and-white paint and he loves attention. Wouldn't you like to ride him?"

He looked angry and hopeless at the same time and then his bottom lip thrust forward and began to tremble. "Yeah. But I don't want to fall off."

Easing her arm around the child's slender shoulders, she said, "Look, Tyler, it's okay to be scared. I know just how you feel."

"I doubt it," he mumbled. "I'll bet you didn't wear any ol' brace like this."

"No. But I once had to wear a cast on my arm for a long time. And at first I was very sad about it. Because I was afraid to ride my horse. His name was Rusty and I loved him more than anything, but I was sure if I got on him I'd fall and break my arm all over again."

Interest sparked in the child's brown eyes. "So what did you do?"

"My father finally reminded me that Rusty was special. The horse was my best friend and he understood that he needed to take extra care of me and not go too fast or make sharp turns. My father told me that if I couldn't trust my best friend, then I would be scared of all sorts of things for the rest of my life. So I decided I wasn't going to let a cast on my arm make me scared or ruin my fun."

Tyler digested this, then thoughtfully tilted his head to one side. "Yeah, but Cloudwalker ain't my friend," he pointed out. "He don't even know me."

"Not yet. But he'd like to make friends with you. And he's like Rusty, he's a very special horse. You can trust him to take care of you. I promise."

"Say, what is this? Are you giving my girl a hard time?"

Both Tyler and Lass turned their heads to see Brady had walked up behind them. He was still dressed in his uniform, but she was grateful to see he'd considered the children and put away his handgun and holster.

Lass rose to her feet to greet him and he quickly slipped his arm around her waist and gathered her to his side. As she smiled at him, she couldn't stop her heart from jumping with joy or stop it from thinking how right it felt to be wrapped in the sheltered circle of his arm.

Rather than appearing intimidated, Tyler surprised her by taking the offensive. "Who says she's your girl?"

"I do. That's who," Brady shot back at him.

Backing down, Tyler mumbled, "Oh. Well, I wasn't tryin' to steal her from you or anything."

"That's good to know. For a minute there I thought you were giving her the eye." Brady gave Lass a discreet little wink. "So why aren't you riding...uh, what did you say your name was? Jim-Bob? Frankie?"

The child rolled his eyes. "No! It's Tyler!"

"Okay, Ty. So why aren't you riding? Think you're better than all the other kids? Or are you afraid you'll fall off and everyone will laugh at you?"

Lass very nearly gasped, but stopped just short of it. Clearly, Brady understood what it was like to be a little boy of Tyler's age. He ought to know how to handle the child better than she. But wasn't he being a little tough?

She didn't have to wonder for long. Tyler instantly hopped off the bale of hay and squared around to face Brady.

"I ain't afraid to ride any ol' horse here!" he exclaimed. "And I won't fall off, either! I'm just as good a cowboy as you are!"

Chuckling now, Brady reached out and affectionately ruffled the child's hair. "Probably better. Now come on and show me what you're made of. Guts or sawdust?"

Tyler thrust his little stomach forward and pointed to the pouch he'd made. "I've got plenty of guts! See! I'll show ya!"

"I can't wait," Brady dared.

Tyler tugged on Lass's sleeve. "Come on, Miss Lass. Let's go get Cloudwalker!"

With a groan and a grin, Lass shook her head. "Male mentality. I don't understand it."

Ten minutes later, Tyler was in the saddle and insisting he could take the reins and handle the horse on his own.

Brady lifted the bridle reins over the paint's head and placed them in Tyler's hands. After a few last-minute instructions, he said, "Okay, off you go. And if you need me or Miss Lass we'll be right here."

"I won't," he said, then confidently set the horse in forward motion.

Standing at one end of the arena, Lass and Brady watched him slowly clop toward the rest of the children.

"Well, I guess he showed you he had guts," she said.

Brady chuckled. "Yes. But you'd already talked him into facing his fears. I just put the rest in motion."

She glanced at him. "I didn't know you heard my story."

"I'd been standing there longer than you think. You've got a pretty good imagination. At least, it worked on Tyler."

Her brows arched. "Imagination? I'll have you know that was a true story."

It was Brady's turn to look surprised. "Really? You actually broke your arm and had a horse named Rusty?"

"Yes. And my father did tell me those things about facing my fears." With a helpless sigh, she pinched the bridge of her nose. "It's crazy, isn't it? I can remember those sorts of things yet I can't remember names or where I lived—except that I believe it was somewhere in Texas."

"Your memory is returning, though. You're recalling more and more. Who knows, in a few days everything may come back to you."

"You could be right," Lass murmured. Each day that passed brought more and more snippets of her past to mind. Bridget called them small signs that her memory was healing. So why didn't that idea bring her more joy? Because she didn't want to face her past? Or because she didn't want to leave this man? A man she'd already fallen in love with?

"Lass, this horse, Rusty, can you remember where you got him? What he looked like?"

Her forehead puckered as she contemplated his questions. "Not exactly. He was sorrel with a long flaxen mane and tail. And I think he had a blaze down his face."

"What about a brand?"

She glanced at him. "A brand?"

"Yes. It's a long shot, but if he had a brand we might trace his ownership."

"I see." She closed her eyes and tried to picture her beloved childhood friend more clearly. "I think—I'm not sure, but I seem to remember there was something on his left hip. Something like an initial. Like a—a *P*. Yes, it was a *P!*"

Encouraged, he nodded. "Good. That's a start. But I doubt one single letter would be used for a brand. It would need a distinguishing mark with it. Like a Bar or Rafter. Rocking. Wings for Flying P. Does any of that ring a bell?"

For several moments, she rolled those possibilities around, then shook her head. Brady was trying so hard to move her case forward. She didn't want to disappoint him. And yet when he asked her to try to remember, her mind recoiled. Dear God, she felt torn in all directions.

"None of that sounds right," she told him. "But I'll try to remember. I promise."

"Don't worry about it, Lass. We still have more options to put into motion."

He glanced thoughtfully out at the children who were presently riding in an obedient circle over the tilled ground. Following his gaze, Lass was happy to see that Tyler was already mixing with the other children, and from the smile on his young face, appeared to have forgotten all about the brace on his leg.

"Since we've been busy with Tyler, I haven't had a chance to tell you yet," he said. "This afternoon, before I left headquarters, I obtained a bit more information about your case."

Lass suddenly froze. "Information? From where? Whom?"

"A jockey. He'd been riding at Ruidoso Downs earlier that Sunday afternoon on the day you were injured. Seems this jockey recalls seeing you at the track that day."

Her heart leaped with something akin to fear. So it was now confirmed. She had been at the local racetrack before she'd been injured.

"Why is the jockey just now coming forward with this information?" she asked, her mind swirling with confusion. "Does he know me personally?"

Brady frowned at her last question. "Why, no. Should he? I mean, do you think in your past that you might have rubbed shoulders that closely with people in the racing circle?"

Tormented by the empty spaces in her mind, she looked at him. "I can't explain it, Brady. It's impossible for me to recall my parents' name, or mine for that matter, but these past few days I've come to realize that I can name every racetrack in the southwest and most of their leading riders, including Ruidoso Downs. I even recall visiting most of the tracks. That has to mean that I was closely associated with the business somehow. But if that's true, then someone should have recognized me before now——before this jockey. Oh, Brady, this is crazy, I know. I'm crazy!"

"Lass!" he gently scolded, "don't ever say that about yourself. You've had an injury and you can't remember everything. That doesn't mean you've lost your mind. There could be all sorts of explanations why no one has recognized you," Brady reasoned. "Could be you've been away from the business for a few years. Or your appearance has changed. That's not uncommon with young women changing their hair color or style. I've had Liam asking around his racing circles to see if anyone has been reported missing, but no one he contacted knows you. But then if you were associated with quarter horses or standard breds he wouldn't be familiar with you or your connections."

She let out a heavy sigh and tried her best to smile at him. "That's true. And I'm sorry, Brady for being so negative. Please—go on about this jockey."

"Well, he says that after the meet that Sunday, he flew out to California to ride at Hollywood Park. He didn't return until yesterday and that's when he saw your picture posted in the clubhouse."

"And out of a crowd of thousands, he remembers seeing me? That sounds highly unlikely."

He continued on in a patient voice, "Lass, you were supposedly standing outside of the saddling paddock just where the horses start onto the track for the post parade. He says he remembers this because his mount tossed him to the dirt right in front of you and he was naturally a little embarrassed about losing his seat in front of an attractive young woman."

Jockeys often lost their seat in the saddle, she thought. It wasn't like that would have been a major occurrence. Still, with it happening right in front of her, she should be able to remember the incident. And yet, she couldn't even recall being at the track that day. "Did he have any other information that might help identify me?"

The corners of Brady's mouth curved downward. "Not exactly. But he does recall that a man was with you. The jockey described this man as being tall, dark-haired and somewhere in his mid- to late-twenties. This new information doesn't necessarily move our case forward," he added, "but it underscores everything that Johnny Chino uncovered. I believe this man at the track is the same man you struggled with on the mountain highway."

Inside her, fear and confusion roiled like a black cloud. She felt suffocated and shaken. "Oh, God, Brady, who was that man?" With both hands, she reached for his arm and clung to him tightly. "Why was I at the track with someone who wanted to…hurt me?"

"Lass, have you ever stopped to think you didn't want to be there with him?"

Her brows pulled together. Could that have happened? Or had she been with this man because she'd wrongly trusted him?

Oh, come on, Lass. It was just a kiss. You know you liked it. Show me again, baby, show me how much you want me.

Suddenly an image was exploding behind her eyes and in it the man's lips were grinding down on hers, bruising, hurting, repulsing her in every way. She pushed hard against his chest and turned to run.

"Lass? Honey, what's wrong?"

Brady's hand stroked her upper arm as Lass struggled to jerk her thoughts back to the present.

"I— Nothing is wrong," she said in a strained voice.

"Nothing! You're trembling, Lass." He wrapped his hand firmly around her elbow. "I want you to go to Dallas's office and lie down on the couch. I'll see after Tyler and the rest of the kids."

Shaking her head, she suddenly set her jaw with determination. Before her accident a man had been trying to manipulate her. She was certain of that now. But who and why? Why had he been kissing her and why had she hated his very touch? Clearly, he was a part of those bad things she'd been running from. And was still running from. Sooner or later, she was going to have to turn and face the shadowy man. Face everything she'd left behind.

"I'm okay, Brady. And I really don't want to talk about this anymore." She pulled her elbow from his grasp. "I'm going to check on the children."

As she walked away, Brady didn't try to stop her. But he desperately wanted to. There was something troubling her. Something more than having to accept that another human being had tried to harm her. He almost got the feeling that a part of her didn't want him to solve the mystery of her identity.

But then, a part of him didn't want to solve it, either.

Chapter Ten

On certain days of the week, Dallas kept the stables open and running so that working parents could bring their children after work hours. But the next evening wasn't a day with extended hours, which allowed Lass to return to the ranch house well in advance of dinnertime. After showering and changing into a peach-colored sundress and a pair of sandals, she started down the stairs with plans to head to the family room.

Normally Kate was the first one there to drink a glass of wine and play her beloved piano. During these past weeks Lass had been on the Diamond D, she'd grown close to the older Donovan woman. Kate was gruff and forward in many ways, but there was a calm strength to the woman that comforted Lass.

"Now this is what I call perfect timing. And you're even dressed for the part."

Hearing Brady's voice, Lass glanced up to see him standing at the foot of the stairs. Apparently he'd been home long enough to change out of his uniform. A pair of worn jeans hugged his thighs and hips while a navy blue T-shirt was tucked into the lean waistband. He looked handsome and sexy, yet it was the warm smile on his face that drew her to him, touched her just as deeply as his kiss.

"Hello, Brady," she greeted, her heart booming in her chest. "I wasn't expecting to see you. Last night at the stables, you said your schedule was changing and that you'd be working late."

She stepped off the bottom stair and he immediately pressed a kiss to her cheek and slung his arm through hers.

"My schedule changed at the last minute. I'm going to a party. Sheriff's orders. And I want you to come along with me."

Unconsciously her palm flattened against her chest. "Me? But I don't know the sheriff, Brady. And I—" biting her lip, she glanced awkwardly away from him "—I really don't want to discuss my case with a…group of strange people."

He gave her arm a reassuring squeeze. "Trust me, honey, there won't be any talk about work. Not from me or the sheriff. If anyone else brings up your situation and you don't want to talk about it, then tell them to mind their own business."

"Oh, Brady," she lightly scolded. "That would be rude and uncomfortable."

"Listen, beautiful, what would be rude and uncomfortable is for you to make me to go to the party tonight without a date. Especially when I was counting on you."

A wry smile of surrender touched her lips. How could she say no to him, when every cell in her body wanted to be with the man? Since that night she'd remembered her mother's death, their relationship had taken a different turn. He seemed to be more gentle, more concerned about her feelings. And whenever he kissed her, it was more than fiery lust. Now when their lips met, she tasted tender passion, felt emotions gently knocking on her heart and begging to come in. If he was seeing other women while he was away from the ranch, she didn't know. Nor did she feel she had the right to question him. But deep down, whenever he looked at her, touched her, she wanted to believe she was special to him. More special than any other woman had been to him.

"All right. I suppose I can go. But what about dinner with your family? And—" she glanced doubtfully down at her dress "—am I dressed appropriately for this outing?"

"Forget dinner with the folks. We'll be eating at the Hamiltons. Their twin boys are turning twelve this week and they're having a little family celebration."

"Oh. And you're considered family? Or was the rest of the sheriff's staff invited, too?" she asked.

The impish grin on his face told Lass that he and the sheriff were closer than he wanted his coworkers to know.

"Some of them will be there. The rest had to stay behind and work." He gestured up to the second floor where the bedrooms were located. "If you want to take a purse or anything, now would be the time to get it. We need to be leaving."

She rolled her eyes. "You believe in giving a girl plenty of notice, don't you?"

He winked. "Gives her less time to back out on me," he teased.

Sure, Lass thought, as she hurried up the stairs to fetch her purse. She doubted Brady had ever been stood up by any woman. And here she was falling over herself to have an outing with the man. What did that say about her? That she was gullible? Vulnerable? Foolish? Or all three? The answer hardly mattered, she told herself. Her resistance had crumbled the moment she'd looked up to see him at the foot of the stairs, smiling as though she was the only woman in his life.

The Hamilton ranch, the Bar H Bar, was located several miles east of Carrizozo, the little county seat where the sheriff's department was located. Just as the sun was setting, Brady drove slowly through an open mesa covered with creosote, grama grass and blue sage. Here and there, prickly pear and cholla cacti grew at the road's edge. Some of the pear cactus was in bloom and the bright yellow roses reminded her of some distant place in her mind, a place where the sun was hot and horse's hooves thundered over a plowed track, giant live oaks spread like deep green umbrellas, shading the lawns and pastures with their sheltering arms.

Home. Was that her home? The snatches of memory caused a part of her heart to ache with longing. Yet when she turned her gaze upon Brady, she realized the thought of leaving him made her ache even more.

"You've gone quiet, Lass. What are you thinking?" Brady asked as he steered the truck over the graveled road. "Are you nervous about meeting my friends?"

By now the mesa was behind them and they were traveling into a group of low-rising hills. Juniper and pinyon dotted the desert slopes while spiny yucca plants dared to grow between slabs of rock.

"A little," she admitted. "But I was mostly thinking how beautiful this land is. How different it is where I came from."

He darted a sharp glance at her. "You're sure about that?" he asked, then grimaced. "Sorry. I forgot that you didn't want to talk about your amnesia this evening."

"It's not a pleasant topic," she said flatly. "But I'm beginning to see that it's a subject I can't avoid entirely. Everything I look at, think about, talk about, connects to my memory. I'm beginning to think I've lost the most important part of my brain."

"You're going to get it back, Lass. I'm as sure of that as I'm sure my middle name is Roark."

Turning slightly in the seat, she studied him instead of the darkening landscape. "Well, to answer your earlier question, yes, I'm sure I didn't live in a desert area. But I'm fairly certain I've been to New Mexico before. It all feels familiar to me now. But then maybe that's because your family has made me feel so at home."

"I'm glad," he said, then slanted a look her way. "And as for my friends, Lass, don't worry about them. They're all just plain folks like us Donovans."

There was nothing plain about the Donovans, she thought. Especially Brady. On the surface he appeared to be a lighthearted, easygoing guy, but that was only one slice of the man. She'd seen it that night he'd found her in the ditch, when he'd stood over her hospital bed and held her hand. And last night, when he'd helped her with Tyler, she'd known he was doing it from his heart and not just for effect.

"I doubt you've ever been described as plain," she said to him. "Why, I even bet in high school you dated the football homecoming queen or the captain of the cheerleading squad, didn't you?"

"Me? Not hardly. Those sorts of girls were too conceited for my taste. They'd rather look at themselves than at me."

Smiling now, Lass glanced curiously over to him. "I'm shocked. So what sort of girls did you go for? I won't believe you if you say the studious type."

He pulled a playful face at her. "Actually, I did have a

studious girlfriend once. She was an honor student. Unfortunately she liked boys as much as she liked getting straight A's. She was a fickle little thing."

"Hmm." She gave him a furtive peek from the corner of her eye. "So what sort of girls do you like now?"

"Oh, that's easy enough to answer. I like the kind of girl who can't remember her own name."

It took a few seconds for the meaning of his words to sink in and then she began to laugh.

Chuckling with her, Brady reached for her hand and as their fingers entwined, she wondered how she could feel so warm and happy at a time like this. Someone had tried to injure or kill her. She didn't know who she was or where she belonged. Yet as long as she was with Brady she could laugh and hope and dream.

She was falling in love with him. To admit it to herself was somewhat of a relief. But to admit it to him would be something altogether different. To reveal her feelings to him now would either draw the two of them closer, or pull them apart. And she was desperately scared of either outcome.

Thankfully, the party at the Hamiltons' proved to be big enough that she didn't have to spend a lot of time making one-on-one conversation with Brady's friends and acquaintances. Instead, he squired her from one group to the next with hardly a chance to make more than small talk.

The twins, Jacob and Jason, were a polite, good-looking pair and at the age where they weren't quite sure if they were still rowdy boys or know-it-all teenagers.

Clearly, their parents understood them, and after the children and adults had partaken of a big barbecue spread, the twins and their young guests were excused to the barn, where they were going to have their own little party.

Penny, their mother, told Lass that the twins' idea of fun was a bucking barrel, a churn of homemade ice cream and a group of girls to watch while the boys made fools of themselves.

Later that evening as Lass sat with their hostess on the edge of a large patio, sipping punch from a paper cup, she commented, "It must be a labor of love to raise twin boys."

Smiling, the dark-haired woman nodded. "They're a handful, but more than worth it."

Three hours had passed since the party first started and now all the adult guests had departed, except for Lass and Brady. While she and Penny enjoyed the quietness, Brady and the sheriff had disappeared into the house. In spite of him assuring Lass that work wouldn't be discussed, she figured that's exactly what the two men were doing. And she wondered if the sheriff might have uncovered something about her case, but hadn't wanted to say anything in front of her.

God, she hoped not. Tonight she simply wanted to pretend that her name really was Lass and that she belonged here. With Brady.

"Brady tells me you're expecting another baby soon," Lass said to the other woman. He'd also revealed to Lass that Penny had once been the county judge for Lincoln County, a position she'd held up until the twins had been born. Since then, the woman worked at her own private law practice.

Penny's eyes glowed as she smiled at Lass. "That's right. I gave birth to the twins shortly before Christmas during a snowstorm." She patted her slightly rounded tummy. "This one is supposed to arrive a little after New Year's and I'm hoping that this time a blizzard won't come with it."

How wonderful that would be, Lass thought, to be having a child with a man you were madly in love with, to plan together for its arrival. Instinctively her hand settled against her own flat midsection.

Now that she'd had plenty of time to think about it, she believed Bridget that she'd never gone through the miraculous experience of childbirth. Yet she knew that having a child was something she'd always longed for. But had there been a man to make that wish come true? No. She refused to believe she'd been madly in love with a man before she'd met Brady. As far as she was concerned, Brady was the first and the last man to step into her heart.

"Do you know if you're going to have twins again?" Lass asked.

Penny laughed. "Oh, dear. That's something Ethan and I have been thinking about. Ethan wants a pair of girls. But the doctor says he can't yet discern whether there are two."

Smiling, Lass told her, "I'll keep my fingers crossed that you'll get those girls."

Playfully wrinkling her nose, Penny leaned forward and said in a low, conspiring tone, "To be honest, I wouldn't know what to do with little girls. I love having rough and tumble sons. But I guess I could learn how to tie ribbons and fix ponytails."

The two women shared a chuckle and then Penny said in a more serious voice, "Brady tells me you've been helping Dallas at the stables."

"That's right. And I'm loving every minute of being with the children," Lass admitted.

"Then I'm sure that someday you'll be like me," Penny replied. "With a house full of kids and more on the way. "

Could Lass allow herself to dream about such things? she wondered. And more important, would Brady want to be a part of those dreams?

You're being very foolish, Lass. Brady is thirty years old and from what his family says, he's shown no interest in getting married or having children. He's not even been engaged. He's not thinking of you in those terms. Besides, you might already have a husband somewhere. A husband who wanted to hurt you.

Doing her best to push away the dark, mocking voice in her mind, she smiled wanly. "I hope you're right, Penny. But until that day comes I'm happy helping Dallas. Kids and horses. It's a combination I can't resist."

She couldn't resist Brady, either, Lass thought with a heavy dose of unease. From the moment she'd opened her eyes and seen his face hovering over hers, she'd felt a sudden connection. And with each day, each hour that passed, that connection continued to deepen.

How soon would it be, she wondered sickly, before that man in her past, the man with the repulsive kiss, showed up on the Diamond D and put an end to all her hopes and dreams?

Later that night, on the way home, Brady was mostly quiet and Lass was content to lean her head back and let her thoughts stray to nothing in particular. But by the time he turned the truck onto Diamond D property, she was beginning to get the sense that something was wrong.

"Brady," she asked, as he let the two of them into the house, "have I…done something wrong? Did I embarrass you in some way tonight?"

He curled his arm around the back of her waist as they began to climb the long wooden staircase. "Are you kidding? You were perfect. Everyone loved you. Why would you think such a thing?"

"You haven't said much since we left the Hamiltons'," she reasoned.

"I'm sorry, Lass. I've been a little distracted."

A little, he thought ruefully. Why the hell couldn't he be honest with her? He was downright troubled. And not just because her identity was still a mystery. Tonight, while she'd stood next to him, her slender arm resting casually on his, he'd felt something he'd never felt before. He'd experienced a sweet connection, a contented ease with her company. Those sorts of feelings about a woman had never struck him before and the whole thing had left him more than a little dazed.

"You and Ethan disappeared into the house for a long while. You were talking work, weren't you?"

He released a guilty groan. "I confess. We did talk a little work. Mostly about you."

"Oh, Brady," she wailed under her breath in order not to disturb the sleeping household. "I've been nothing but a headache to you. If I had any sense at all, I'd leave here and let you and your family get some peace."

By now they had reached her bedroom door and he caught her by the upper arms and turned her to face him. "Is that what you really want, Lass? To go off somewhere—to be a charity ward of the county?"

"I'm not helpless. I can work and support myself," she shot back at him, then groaned with regret. "I'm sorry, Brady. I'm sounding very ungrateful and I don't want you to think that. I—" Her hands gently rested against his chest. "No. I don't want to leave here. But I'm—"

"Look, Lass, I haven't mentioned this to you, but after I got the call from the jockey, I made a decision to flood several Texas newspapers with your photo and story. That was early yesterday. Now a few calls and tips are starting to come in and we're trying to sift through them as quickly as we can to see if any are legitimate. So far you've been identified as everything from an elementary teacher in the

Texas panhandle to a PFC in the Texas National Guard and a sales clerk at a Neiman Marcus in Dallas. It will take us a while to confirm if any of the callers actually know you or your family. But I have a gut feeling I'm going to have some answers for you soon."

She looked up at him and through the dim lighting of the landing, he could see turmoil swirling in her gray eyes. To his wonder, she looked exactly the way he was feeling inside.

"And how do you feel about that?" she whispered.

He groaned, then, bending down, he pressed his cheek against hers. "I feel torn, Lass. I don't want anything or anyone to come between us," he murmured against her ear.

She pulled her head back to look at him and as his gaze settled on her lips his gut twisted with a need so great it was almost painful.

"Do you really mean that?" she asked.

"I can't believe you have to ask me that, Lass. Since you've came into my life everything has changed. I've changed. You and me together. That's the most important thing to me now."

Without saying more, he angled his head to kiss her. She tasted soft and sweet and giving, and when her arms slipped up and around his neck and her lips unfolded beneath his, he felt more than pleasure, he felt totally and strangely happy.

Quickly, he deepened the connection of their mouths and just as instantly passion fired, then exploded like flint against rock, flame to dead grass. From somewhere in the core of him, heat spread, then raced outward, downward until desire was gripping his whole body like a red-hot vise. The need to make love to her was searing a hole in his brain, turning every scrap of common sense into useless ashes.

Somehow, he managed to tear his lips from hers and as

he sucked in deep, ragged breaths, he caught her by the hands and tugged her toward the end of the landing, where his bedroom was located.

She followed his lead, but whispered as they went, "Brady, what are you doing? My bedroom is…behind us."

Opening a carved wooden door, he flipped a switch and a small lamp at the head of the bed instantly shed a shaft of soft yellow light across a dark blue spread.

"But this is where we're going," he explained. "To my room."

She didn't say anything until they were standing inside the dark room and he'd locked the door securely behind them.

"Brady! This is risky! What if someone comes to your room?"

With his hands against the back of her waist, he groaned and pulled her close. "In the middle of the night? No chance. No one ever disturbs me. Besides, the door is locked. The two of us are finally alone and together."

"Together," she repeated wondrously, then shyly pressed her cheek against his. "Oh, Brady, I do want us to be together."

Her softly spoken words filled him with an urgency he could hardly contain. Swiftly, he picked her up in his arms and carried her over to the bed. After he'd laid her in the middle of the wide mattress, then stretched out beside her, he framed her face with his hands and simply gazed at her, letting his eyes fill with the lovely sight of her.

"Why are you looking at me like…I'm strange?" she whispered.

The corners of his mouth tilted, his eyes gentled. "*Strange* is the wrong word, Lass. Try special. I've never seen a woman lying in my bed before. I didn't realize it would look this good. Feel this right."

Between the loose hold of his fingers, her head twisted

back and forth. "Don't talk to me as though I'm naive, Brady. I know you've had other women in your bed."

One hand slipped to the back of her neck and pulled her face forward so that their eyes and lips were level and only scant inches apart. Her heart was pounding and she must have forgotten how to breathe because her lungs were burning almost as much as the rest of her body.

"Lass, my little Lass, you misunderstand. Yes, I've had a woman in *a* bed before. But not *my* bed. *This* bed. Since I was a small boy, this is where I've always slept. It's my private place where I rest and dream and, these past few weeks, pictured you in my arms. Now here you are and I can't look at you enough. Can't touch you enough."

He closed the last bit of space between their lips and as the connection deepened, she groaned softly and rolled toward him. With his mouth fastened hungrily to hers, he gathered the front of her body close to his, then his hands went on a reckless exploration across her back, down her hips, then up to the small curve of her breasts. The dress she was wearing zipped in the back and his fingers trembled as he searched for the handle, then slowly tugged the fastener downward.

Beneath the tough pads of his fingers, her skin felt like satin and when he slipped the piece of fabric off her shoulder and bent his head to the curve of her neck, it tasted like smooth cream sweetened with sugar.

As a lawman he'd always thought of himself as a protector, but with Lass in his arms the feeling intensified a thousand times over. He wanted to shelter her, worship her, bind her to him so closely that nothing or no one could touch her or tear her from him.

Savoring the fine texture of her skin, his lips moved across her throat, then upward to the tender spot beneath her chin. He could feel her soft sighs brushing his cheeks, the beat of her heart pounding against his, her hands gliding over his shoulders and across his back.

The need to feel those hands against him, to have her slender fingers playing over his bare skin, was so fierce he drew back from her and quickly began to deal with the buttons on his shirt. Lass followed his cue and while he shrugged out of his shirt, she pushed her dress over her hips and allowed it to fall to the floor.

The sight of her wearing nothing but pink lace caused blood to pound in his ears, his loins. His body was screaming to make love to her, yet at the same time his mind was gearing down, commanding his hands and lips to linger, to investigate and memorize every curve, every inch and every pore of her heated skin.

Up until this moment, Lass hadn't really understood what being lost meant. With her lips consumed by his, her body turning to soft putty in his hands, she was as lost as a raindrop falling into a wide, dark ocean. He was her only anchor and she clung to him, her mouth a willing prisoner to his as he kissed her over and over, while his tongue tangled, plunged and teased.

By the time he pulled away from her and began to deal with the rest of his clothing, Lass's body had become a heated coil, winding itself tighter and tighter until every cell in her body felt as though it would explode.

Shamelessly, her breaths coming hard and fast, she removed the last flimsy remnants of her clothing and waited for him to rejoin her on the bed. When he finally turned back to her, she could see that he'd already taken care of protection and for one split second, the reality of what they were about to do whooshed like a chilly breeze through her mind. But that one brief second ended as soon as his hands reached for her, then pressed her back upon the mattress.

Stretching next to her side, he spoke against her cheek. "From the first time I kissed you, I've wanted you like this."

Her hands left his shoulders to gently frame his face and he paused to gaze into her eyes.

"And I've wanted you," she murmured.

A soft, inviting light flickered in her eyes and he felt something in the middle of his chest jerk, then like a broken fountain, emotions flowed unchecked, drowning him, terrifying him with their intensity.

"Lass," he uttered hoarsely. "My Lass."

It was all he could say as his throat closed together and his arms instinctively tightened around her.

Tilting her head back, she offered her lips up to his and this time when he kissed her, his body won the war over his mind. He could no longer slow this trip they were taking. He needed her. All of her. Nothing else could quench the violent force driving his movements.

Beneath him, her legs parted with invitation, and with one smooth thrust he sank into her soft wetness. As her warmth surrounded him, pleasure such as he'd never experienced wrapped around him, snapped his head back and momentarily paralyzed his movements.

And then he felt her hips thrusting toward his, her back bowing, crushing her breasts against his chest. With a guttural growl of desperation, he began to move inside her and with each exquisite thrust he felt himself falling, tumbling to a place he'd never been before.

Beneath him, Lass tried to keep up with his frantic pace, tried to knead, touch, taste every bump and hollow on his hard, muscled body. Like a strong wine, she wanted to drink him, savor every taste, every magical sensation that was intoxicating her senses.

Soon she was gasping for air and the need inside was clawing at her like a fierce cat, hissing, twitching, readying itself for the final pounce. When that final leap came, she swallowed her cries and gripped him close. And like water over a fall, she was suddenly flowing wild and free, drifting languidly, until finally she ebbed onto a soft, sandy shore.

The second Brady felt her velvety softness tightening around him, heard the low, keening moan deep in her throat, he lost all touch with his surroundings. Unbearable pleasure burst inside him, flung him upward and outward until he was sure his heart had split open and everything it held was spilling into her.

The urge to shout was so great that he buried his face into the curve of her neck and kept it there until the shudders in him subsided.

Once the walls of the room quit spinning, Brady realized he was sprawled over Lass and she was supporting the brunt of his weight. Quickly, he rolled to one side of her and lying flat against the mattress, stared in stunned wonder at the shadowed ceiling.

So that was making love, he thought. He'd not known or ever imagined that such give and take could go on between a man and a woman. She'd taken him over a precipice, and even if he'd known the fall would kill him, he still would have gone willingly, happily.

Somewhere from the dark corners of his mind, fear pricked like a cold, evil blade and he turned his head to look at her.

At that moment, she rolled to face him and strands of her long black hair spilled over a flushed cheek and swung a modest curtain over one breast. Her lips were dark pink and puffy, her skin covered with a sheen of sweat. He'd never seen anything so lovely, so perfect. And though he'd not yet caught his breath, he felt desire stir in him all over again.

Shifting toward her, he reached out and gently tucked the errant strands of hair behind her ear.

"What are you thinking?" he asked gently.

The corners of her mouth tilted wanly and then to his dismay, her gray eyes glazed, then pooled with tears.

"I think," she whispered huskily, "that I love you, Brady Donovan."

Chapter Eleven

I love you. Those three little words were the last thing Brady expected to hear from Lass. For a second time tonight she'd stunned him and as he gazed at her, his thoughts were spinning, searching for a way to reply that wouldn't make him sound insensitive or patronizing or, God help him, an enchanted fool.

In spite of his reputation for having racked up more dates than Abe Cantrell had cattle, Brady had never had a woman tell him she loved him. Well, maybe once in high school, but that had been from a silly little drama student, who'd not really known the meaning of the word, but truly believed she was destined for a star on the Hollywood walk of fame. So as far as he was concerned that one time hadn't counted.

But tonight, with Lass, he'd felt the emotion in her voice, saw a glow in her eyes that made him feel amazed, yet at the same time terribly unworthy. She deserved the best. She deserved to be loved in return. But was he capable of that?

His hand trembling, he trailed his fingertips down her damp cheek. "Lass, I don't know what to say. I—"

Her forefinger touched his upper lip, stopping anything else he might have said. "You don't have to say anything," she gently insisted. "I don't expect you to tell me that you love me back."

She scooted closer to him and the musky, womanly scent of her swirled around him, caught his senses and sent them dancing away to hide in a shadowy corner. Then just as he was trying to drag them back, her hand drifted onto his shoulder and glided down his arm. Her touch scattered goose bumps across his skin.

"I just...thought you should know how I feel," she went on, then with a sigh, she pressed her cheek against his chest. "That's all."

His throat thickened, his eyes closed. Was that his heart tearing down the middle? Did love feel like a fist punching him in the gut, making his whole chest ache? If so, then he was scared. Scared that the pain might never stop.

"Lass, maybe...what you're really feeling for me is gratitude. Because I found you—that night on the road."

An objective groan sounded in her throat. "Look, Brady, I'm grateful to anyone who helps me. And I may not remember my own name, but I don't believe that I ever went around thanking the men in my life like—" she reared her head back to look at him "—like this."

"God, I hope not."

She slanted him a wry look. "I should have never said anything to you about my...feelings. Now you're uncomfortable and I don't know how to put you at ease, to convince you that I'm not expecting vows or pledges or flowery words from you. I'm not blind. I can see that you don't want to be serious about any woman."

He was shocked at how much of him was insulted by her not so flattering assessment. "Really?" he asked sardonically. "You can see that about me, through all the muddy conceit and selfishness?"

Disappointment filled her eyes and Brady was suddenly ashamed of himself. He didn't know what was pushing him to say such things. It must be that odd pain in his chest that was putting words in his mouth.

Sighing, she rolled away from him and climbed from the bed. Confused, Brady watched her walk over to the nearest window and stare out at the dark, moonless sky. And though the lovely sight of her nakedness was riveting, it was the wistful expression on her face that caught his attention and pushed him to leave the bed and go stand behind her.

Sliding his arms around her waist, he bent his head and pressed a kiss to her bare shoulder. Her skin was warm and salty and he had to catch himself before his teeth began to nibble, his hands lift to cup her breasts.

"I'm sorry, Lass. I guess I'm not saying anything right."

"Maybe it would be better if you didn't say anything at all," she suggested, her voice painfully distant.

Lifting his head, he rested his chin on the top of her head. "I can't do that, Lass. I want you to understand that… well, you threw me for a loop."

Twisting in his arms, she looked up at him, her gaze searching. "Why?"

Grimacing, he shook his head. "I don't know. Lass, this is all new for me. I don't know what being in love feels like and I've never dated any woman long enough to give her the chance to fall in love with me."

"Why?" she asked again.

Her simple question pulled a groan from his throat.

"This is probably going to sound corny to you, but to me love means forever. It's like marriage—once you do it, it ought to be for life."

Her gray eyes suddenly softened. "Is that why you've not yet loved or married? Because you don't want to be connected to someone for life?"

With a rough sigh, he pulled her to him and cradled her head against his shoulder. As his fingers meshed in the silky strands of her hair, he asked, "Did you know that both of my brothers have been married?"

"Yes. Kate told me that Conall is divorced and Liam is widowed."

"That's right. Conall was married for a few years and then things went wrong between him and his wife. Liam's wife was killed in a car accident. She was pregnant with their first child at the time."

Lass gasped. "Oh, how tragic!"

"Yeah. Both my brothers have endured too much heartache."

Her gaze sharpened on his face. "So you're afraid to try love or marriage? Afraid that tragedy will strike you, too?"

"Not exactly," he answered, then his mouth twisted wryly. "Funny you should think that about me. My family tends to think I'm a shallow fellow when it comes to women. That I'm some sort of heartbreaker." Snorting softly, he shook his head. "I guess to them it does look that way. I have to admit that I've dated plenty of women over the years, but I don't have anything against love or marriage. It's just something…well, I want to be cautious about it. I need a woman strong enough to cope with my job, with the worries and fears, and realize that I truly want to keep being a deputy. A lot of the girls I dated couldn't really cope with the hours and the schedule and the job. And I want to get a little older and wiser before I take the plunge and then maybe I'll have a marriage like my parents have."

Her palms rested upon chest. "And that's what you want, a marriage like your parents'?"

His fingers stroked the silky hair lying upon her shoulder. "I want a woman I can love. The way my dad loves my mother. The way my grandpa loved my grandma. What they had, what my parents have now, is that forever kind of thing. Nothing can rattle it or break it. That's what I want. And I'm not going to make a vow to God to love, honor and obey, unless I can truly mean it."

One corner of her mouth slowly curved upward. "Why, Brady, I never suspected you of being such an old-fashioned sort of guy."

Her arms were sliding around his waist, her warm little body leaning into his and that in itself was enough to put a smile on his face. "Is that what you call it? Mom calls it being too particular," he said, then brushing his knuckles against her cheek, he added thickly, "But I'm beginning to think you're absolutely perfect—for me."

"Oh, Brady, I—"

"Shh. Let's not waste any more of this night talking," he gently interrupted. "Morning will be here soon enough."

Apparently, she agreed with him. Without another word, she rose on tiptoes and fastened her mouth over his. And as desire for her began to burn all over again, Brady was content to let his mind go blank and ignore the restless questions in his heart.

The next morning, Brady had to be at work early, but thankfully not as early as most mornings when he headed to Carrizozo long before daylight. When the alarm finally jolted him awake, he expected to see Lass's head on the pillow next to his. Instead, he found himself alone with nothing but memories of the love they'd made in his bed.

The fact that she'd chosen to leave him sometime while he was asleep, stung him a bit. He'd thought their night together had changed everything. He'd thought she'd grown as close to him as he had to her. Maybe he'd presumed too much.

Rolling to his side, he wiped a hand over his face and told himself he was becoming downright maudlin. He couldn't expect Lass to simply stay in his room all night, then go down to breakfast together as though they were a married couple. She had more respect for herself and his family than that. And he had more respect for her than that.

So what do you want, Brady? For her to be your wife? Do you want the right to have her in your bed, your life for always? Is she that woman you've been searching for?

Always. Always was a long time, Brady mused, as he pushed himself out of bed and walked toward his private bathroom. Would having only one woman in his life get boring? Would he regret not being able to play the field?

Something made him suddenly stop in the middle of the room and gaze back at the bed he'd shared with Lass. Nothing about Lass could ever be boring. Even if she was gray and wrinkled he would want her. Love her.

Yes, he could admit it to himself now. But saying those words to Lass were quite another thing. Her past might have already promised her future to someone else. And if that turned out to be the case, what would he do? What could he do?

After a quick shower, he hurried down to the kitchen in hopes of catching Lass before she left with Dallas to work at the riding stables. But when he reached the kitchen, Conall was the only person he found.

Of the three Donovan brothers, Conall was the enigmatic one. With hair as dark as their mother's and eyes as green as an Irish shamrock, he was a handsome devil. Or at least he would be, Brady thought, if he'd find it in himself to smile as though he was enjoying life. But with a natural head for business, that side of the ranch had been handed over to him and with the job came heavy responsibilities. Brady couldn't remember the last time Conall had taken time off for himself or left the ranch for anything more than business.

Dressed in a starched white shirt and dark tie, Conall was sitting at a small breakfast bar located at the end of the cabinets, nursing a cup of coffee and rifling through the *Lincoln County News* when Brady walked into the room.

At the sound of his footsteps, Conall peered over the top of the newspaper, "You're getting around late this morning, aren't you?"

"Not exactly," Brady explained. "Yesterday my schedule changed a bit and I have to work later."

He poured himself a cup of coffee, then peered at the breakfast food that Opal had left in the warming drawer. The eggs and bacon still looked fresh so he helped himself to a plate full, then carried the meal over to a table situated near a sliding plate glass door. Beyond it, he could see his grandmother trimming her roses. The sight comforted him.

"Where is everyone?" he asked.

"In everyone, you mean Lass?"

The faint sarcasm in Conall's voice jerked Brady's head up and he stared sharply at his brother. "Okay, have you seen Lass this morning?"

"She and Dallas have already left for the stables. You

should have gotten up earlier if you'd planned on kissing her goodbye."

Brady's jaw tightened. He and Conall had always been as different as daylight and dark, but they normally got along well. He didn't know why his brother was being so testy this morning, but he was hardly in the mood for it.

"What is that supposed to mean?"

Laying the paper to one side, his brother looked squarely at him. "Oh, come on, Brady, the whole family can see you've fallen for the girl. What have you done, turned into some sort of idiot?"

Falling in love with Lass made him an idiot? For an instance, Brady reverted to his childhood and wanted to jump up from the table and wrench Conall's arm around his back and twist until his brother took back every word he'd just said. But the days where they'd physically fought had ended years ago. Now that they were grown men, they had to fight with words.

"I ought to knock your damned head off for that," Brady muttered.

Unperturbed, Conall grimaced. "Why get mad just because I struck a nerve? I'm only trying to point out that you're making a mistake."

Even if he'd been starving, at that moment Brady couldn't have wedged a bite of food between his gritted teeth. "Oh, you're an authority on women now? That's a laugh." He jerked up his coffee cup and brought it halfway to his mouth. "Sometimes you're a real bastard, Conall."

Leaving the bar stool, his brother walked over to the small table, jerked out a chair and sank into it.

"Maybe I am a bastard," Conall said in deceptively soft voice, "but I'm just trying to keep you from being hurt."

"Like you?" Brady retorted.

"That's a low blow."

It was a low blow and the realization helped Brady put a lid on his rising temper. He shouldn't have let Conall's remarks get to him. But these past few days he'd been torn between his search for Lass's identity and his growing feelings for her. He was walking a tightrope and his nerves were raw from the strain. Wiping a hand over his face, he said, "I shouldn't have said that. But Lass is…important to me."

"That's the whole point," Conall replied. "You don't know who she is or where she came from. She could be carrying all sorts of trouble or baggage that you don't yet know about. Is that the sort of woman you want to bring into our family?"

At one time, Conall himself had brought a fairly disturbed woman into the family. But Brady wasn't going to point that out. He'd already suffered enough without him bringing up the subject of Conall's ex-wife.

"Lass is a good person. I don't have to run a police check on her to know that."

Rising to his feet, Conall shrugged. "I don't know what the hell I'm worrying about this for. You've never stayed interested in one woman for more than a week or two. Lass will be no different."

Like hell, Brady thought.

Forcing his attention to his plate, he shoveled up a fork full of eggs. "This is one time, big brother, you need to mind your own business."

Without another word, Conall turned and left the room.

For the next four days, Brady was relegated to working the night shift. Which meant he left the ranch while Lass was working at the stables and didn't return home until the middle of the night. She'd talked to him on the phone, but those conversations had been brief and while she'd been in the company of the stables staff. So she'd had little chance to say anything personal, like how much she was missing him, how much she was aching to have his arms back around her. But he'd let her know he'd not forgotten her or their night together. One evening she'd found a fresh flower on her pillow and last evening he'd left a gift wrapped box on her nightstand. Inside had been an ivory lace shawl with a short note telling her the gift was meant to keep her warm until he could wrap his arms around her once again.

She was totally and utterly besotted with the man and these last few days without him had only underscored how empty her life would be without him. The realization was weighing on her, adding to the confusion that continued to swirl through her mind.

Images of her past were coming to her more frequently now and the sights and sounds had grown intense and frightening. Out of the blue, flashes of that day at the Ruidoso track had been striking her, filling her with a sense of unease and then downright horror.

David. It was a man named David who'd been kissing her against her will, shoving her into a car, then chasing her into the mountain ravine. Yet she still couldn't put a last name to his face or what he'd meant to her past life. Then last night as she'd lain in bed, the image of her father had once again floated to the front of her mind. She'd not been able to focus directly on his face, but she'd known the big, towering figure was his. In the vision she'd been shouting at him, swearing that she never wanted to see him again. But why?

Oh, God, had her father tried to hurt her, too? Why had she been so angry with him? Because her mother was dead? Had he done something to her mother? Had Lass been running, trying to escape from David and her father?

If only she could put the pieces of the puzzle together, she thought, then all of her memory might fall into place. But what would that do to her and Brady? She loved him. But she recognized that for him, their relationship was only beginning and he might never love her in return. If her memory returned and she had to leave the Diamond D, the chance for her to earn Brady's love would be over.

"Lass? Are you out here?"

Turning at the sound of Dallas's voice, Lass saw the other woman stepping into the barn where they stored the feed and tack for the children's mounts.

"I'm here," Lass called out to her. "Just putting away a few bridles."

Dallas walked over to her. "The last rider just left," she said. "Are you ready to head for home?"

Lass looped a headstall over a wooden peg, then stepped off a short, wooden platform to join the other woman.

"You mean Tyler has already gone, too? I was going to tell him goodbye."

"His mother picked him up a few minutes ago," Dallas told her, "but I wouldn't worry about it. Tyler knows that you care about him. In fact, I'm amazed at the progress you've made. Once you and Brady got him on Cloud-walker, he's become a different child."

Lass's smile turned a bit dreamy. "Brady is very good with children. Did you know that?"

Dallas laughed. "Not really. I can't remember seeing him with a kid. But apparently my brother has a few hidden talents that his family doesn't know about."

Blushing, Lass glanced away from the other woman's perceptive gaze. "Yes, he does."

Wrapping her arm around Lass's shoulder, Dallas gave

her an encouraging squeeze. "You've been missing him these past few days, haven't you?"

Lass stared at the toes of her boots. "Oh, dear, is it that obvious?"

"You're not the one that's obvious, Lass. Brady is the one who's behaving like a man in love. At least, that's what Grandma thinks and so do I."

Something between a sob and a groan sounded in Lass's throat as she turned and walked to the open doorway of the barn.

Staring out at the distant mountains, she spoke in a heavy voice, "Oh, Dallas, I'm beginning to think I've lost more than my memory. I've lost my mind. I had no business falling in love with your brother. No right at all."

"Why?"

Jerking her head around, she stared in dismay at Dallas. "Do you honestly have to ask?"

Dallas turned her palms upward in an innocent gesture. "Well, yes. You're a young, lovely woman and he's single, employed and manages to keep his fingernails clean. What's wrong with the two of you getting together?"

Groaning with frustration, Lass shoved a hand through her black hair. "Dallas, I've…been remembering things. Bits and pieces of my life before I came here. A man was involved. I don't know who or what he was to me. And then there's my father—I can almost see him, but I can't speak his name. We're arguing terribly and I'm saying awful things to him. Something bad was going on in my life, with my family. I don't know what or why. But it's clear that I can't start any sort of relationship with that sort of baggage hanging over my head."

Tsking her tongue with disapproval, Dallas shook her head. "Lass, bad things happen to all of us from time to time. They can be resolved. And I happen to think that Brady is going to put this puzzle together." She reached for Lass's arm and urged her away from the barn door. "C'mon, honey, and quit worrying. Let's get home. Who knows, Brady might actually show up at the dinner table."

Later that night, Brady and Hank took a break from patrolling the western side of the county to enjoy pie and coffee at the Blue Mesa Café in Ruidoso. It was well past midnight and except for a hippie-looking couple eating burgers, the restaurant was empty.

"Brady, why don't you put those papers down and eat your pie. The whipped cream is melting."

Earlier this evening at headquarters, Brady had printed out a stack of information pertaining to Lass's case and this break was the first chance he'd had to look it over. Now he glanced impatiently across the table to Hank.

"I'm eating," he told the young deputy. To prove his point, he whacked off a piece of the apple pie and jammed it into his mouth.

Grimacing, Hank complained, "For all the company you've been this evening, I might as well have come out on this patrol by myself. Ever since we left headquarters you've been somewhere else."

"I'm working, Hank. Remember, that's what we're supposed to be doing."

"Yeah. One job at a time. You can't patrol and do detective work simultaneously."

Frowning with faint amusement, Brady looked at the junior deputy. "Simultaneously? Where did that come from?"

Hank shot him a bored look. "From the dictionary. Where else? It means at the same time. Like doing reading and eating together."

Brady slapped the tabletop. "Hellfire, I know what simultaneously means! What are you doing using it? It sounds ridiculous."

Hank pursed his lips together. "Ya know, Brady, a guy just can't please you. Remember how you're always gettin' on to me about my grammar? Well, I've been doing something about it. I've been studying the dictionary, building my vocabulary."

Pinching the bridge of his nose, Brady wearily shook his head. "I'm sorry I ever said anything about your grammar."

"Shoot, I ain't. You're only trying to give me a little class. And I figure if I can talk right, I'll be a lot bigger hit with the ladies. Like you."

"Not like me!" Brady blustered under his breath, then with a rueful sigh, reached for his coffee. "You're as bad as my family, Hank. They think I'm incapable of having a serious thought about a woman."

"I didn't say anything like that," Hank defended himself, then with a curious expression leaned toward Brady. "Are you?"

"Shut up. Just shut up and eat," Brady ordered, then snatched up the papers and tried to refocus on the list of names in front of him. He was fishing for one tiny minnow in a huge ocean, he thought wryly. But he had to start somewhere.

"What are you looking at anyway?" Hank asked as he went back to tackling the cherry pie on his plate. "Something to do with that knifing incident last night at the Bull's Head? I thought you'd already handed in that report."

"This is about Lass. It's a list of registered brands in the state of Texas."

Hank rolled his eyes. "Oh, well, that sounds logical. The woman can't remember her name, but she can remember her family's brand. You're reachin', aren't you, partner?"

Brady shot him an annoying glare. "And you're going to be hanging, partner, by your thumbs, if you keep it up."

Hank turned serious. "Sorry, Brady. I'm just thinking about you. You've been worrying me. Ever since we found that gal, you've been different."

Brady realized that this was one time Hank was right. He had been different. Now that Lass had come into his life, nothing felt the same. He wasn't that man who'd taken one day at a time and lived only to work and play. Now he was thinking forward, dreaming, planning, imagining a future with Lass.

But that couldn't happen, he realized, until he knew for certain that she was free to become his. Until she was free from her forgotten past.

"She's become important to me, Hank. And I want to be able to solve this thing, to give her back her real name."

"Or give her yours?" Hank countered.

Brady stared at him. Leave it to Hank to put everything in simple terms, he thought wryly.

"Maybe."

The deputy whistled under his breath. "Boy, you have got yourself in a fix."

"What is that supposed to mean?"

Hank swallowed the last bite of his pie. "Think about it, Brady. You believe a woman who looks like Lass didn't have a man hangin' close? Why, there's probably a husband or fiancé out there right now just combing the countryside for her."

That possibility was the one thing that Brady couldn't shake from his mind. The idea haunted him day and night.

"If that's the case, then why hasn't he shown up to fetch her back home?" Brady asked. "That's what I want to know."

Hank swung his gaze around the empty restaurant, as though he'd find the answers somewhere among the empty tables and booths. "Maybe he don't want to find her. Maybe he wants to keep her danglin' for a while. Just to teach her a lesson."

That idea made Brady's hands curl into fists upon the tabletop. "Only a sick bastard could do that."

"That's why you'd better find him first," Hank wisely replied.

His partner was right, Brady thought, as unease trickled down his spine. The only way he could keep Lass truly safe was to find her true identity. And the only hope he had to keep her in his arms was to hope she loved him more than the man she'd left behind.

Chapter Twelve

The next morning, shortly before lunch, Brady was sitting at his desk, continuing to pour over an endless list of registered Texas brands when he suddenly stumbled across the one he'd been looking for. At least, he believed it could be the one. The letter *P* merged with an *F*.

The brand had been registered some forty years ago by a Francis Porter for Porter Farms. Whether Francis was a man or woman, or whether Porter Farms was still in existence, he didn't yet know. But at least he had something to start with.

In spite of the three short hours of sleep he'd gotten before heading back to work, excitement rushed through him. These past few days, he'd missed Lass terribly and later this evening, he'd be off duty for the next three days. He couldn't wait to see her, hold her, make love to her again. And maybe, God willing, he'd also be able to also give her news about her case.

Ignoring the talk and commotion of the deputies working in the next room, Brady quickly began to search the Internet for anything related to a Porter Farms. Not expecting much, he was amazed when a whole Web site suddenly emerged on the monitor screen.

Porter Farms bred and raised quarter horse racing stock. That explained why Liam or anyone in his thoroughbred circle could identify her. The different breeds raced separately, their auctions were held at different times and places, and most all trainers specialized in one breed. Not both. She wouldn't have traveled in thoroughbred circles. But was this Porter Farms connected to Lass?

Although there was no family photo available, the Web site was full of photos of the ranch and many horses, yearlings, and weanlings presently for sale. It was a professionally done site, offering high class animals. The Porter family had to be rich, he decided. Rich enough to splurge on diamond and turquoise earrings and handmade boots, the sort that Lass had been wearing the night he'd found her lying unconscious on the side of the road.

An address, telephone number and detailed map of the ranch's location were all right there for him to see and Brady's hand shook as he scribbled the information down on a scrap of paper, then reached for the phone.

Surely it couldn't be this easy, he thought.

The phone rang three times before a woman picked it up. She answered in a business-like manner and Brady realized he'd reached the commercial part of the ranch, rather than the private homestead.

"This is Brady Donovan, Chief Deputy of Lincoln County New Mexico," he said, identifying himself. "Could I possibly speak to a family member?"

There was a long pause and then the secretary replied, "Mr. Porter isn't in right now. And Miss Camille is…away."

Miss Camille. Away. Could that be Lass? Brady's heart was suddenly pounding.

"Is that the daughter of the house?" he questioned.

"Yes. Yes, she is. Is this an emergency, Deputy? Is something wrong?"

He'd classify it as worse than an emergency if these people knew that Lass was missing and hadn't lifted a finger to do anything to find her. But why would anyone do such a thing? His teeth clenched.

"Not exactly. Is there another family member I could speak with? A son? Wife perhaps?"

"No. Mrs. Porter passed on a couple of months ago. And there are no sons in the family."

My mother is dead. Even though more than three weeks had passed since Lass had revealed that painful memory to him, he'd not forgotten the stricken sound of her voice, the tears in her eyes. This had to be her home and family or a very uncanny coincidence.

"I see," he said thoughtfully. "Well, could you please have Mr. Porter call me as soon as possible. It's very important."

He gave the woman his own personal cell number, then hung up. As he entered Ethan's office, his mind was spinning, wondering if he would hear from the man or if he'd have to take the investigation to another level. One that could involve the Texas Rangers.

For the next fifteen minutes, he discussed everything he'd discovered with Ethan about Lass's case and had moved on to a stabbing incident that had occurred near Ruidoso two nights ago, when his phone rang.

After a quick glance at the illuminated number, he motioned to Ethan that it was the call he'd been waiting for.

Swallowing away the tightness in his throat, he answered, "Deputy Donovan."

There was a long pause and for a moment Brady feared the connection had been severed, but then a man's voice sounded in his ear.

"This is Ward Porter. My secretary said you wanted to speak with me."

Brady hadn't realized he'd gotten to his feet until he looked down and saw Ethan sitting behind his desk, calmly waiting for him to finish the call.

This time Brady was forced to clear his throat. "That's right. I'm working on a missing persons case. A young woman in her mid-twenties. Black hair. Gray eyes."

"That's Camille—my daughter! But she's not missing."

"Your secretary says she's currently away from home."

"That's right. She went on vacation."

"Where?"

"I don't know. She wouldn't tell me where she was going."

"When was the last time you talked to her?" Brady persisted.

"I'm not sure. Three—no, something like four weeks ago."

The man sounded agitated now and Brady could tell he was holding something back.

"And that doesn't concern you?"

"Well, hell yes, it concerns me! But what's a father to do when his daughter refuses to talk to him? Look, I don't know what this is about, but Camille is wherever she is because she wants to be there. She damned well doesn't want to be on Porter Farms with me! She made that clear enough when she spun out of here in that damned sports car of hers. And the last time I checked it was still at the airport, so apparently she's not flown back into San Antonio."

And why was that, Brady wanted to shout at him.

Instead, he fought to keep his voice and his questions impersonal. He wasn't a judge or juror, he was simply a lawman. And he couldn't allow his love for Lass to interfere with his job.

"You're certain about everything you're telling me?"

There was another long pause and then the man said in a voice that had suddenly turned quiet and confused, "Wait a minute, are you telling me that you have my daughter for some reason? What's happened to her? Is she—"

"The young woman in question doesn't know who she is or where she came from. For the past three weeks or more she's had amnesia. The sheriff's department here is trying to contact anyone who might know her."

"Oh, God. Oh no," the man whispered in a genuinely stricken voice. "How did she get amnesia? Are you sure it's my daughter? That it's Camille?"

"We're not exactly sure what happened. She received a head injury." Brady went on to describe Lass in detail and finished with her apparent affinity for horses. "We do know she was at the racetrack some time before she was injured. Is that something your daughter would normally do?"

"Every chance she got. I—" He suddenly paused and Brady was amazed to hear the man choke up with emotion. If he cared about his daughter that much, why hadn't he made an effort to find her? "I'll be there by tomorrow afternoon," he finished. "Where will I find you?"

Brady gave him directions to the Diamond D, along with a reminder to bring the proper papers to prove his identity and his connection to Lass, then hung up the phone.

Behind the desk, Ethan shook his head. "Sounds like the man has some explaining to do."

"A whole lot of it," Brady muttered. He paced restlessly around the room, then stopped to stare at the sheriff. "You know, for a minute when I found the Web site for Porter Farms I kept thinking how easy this whole thing was. But I was wrong. It hasn't been easy. Nothing about it has been easy. If Lass hadn't remembered that brand on her horse we'd still be at square one. Because this Ward Porter, this man that claims to be her father, wasn't making any effort to find his daughter. He didn't even consider her missing."

Disgusted, Ethan shook his head. "Broken families. Uncaring relatives. In this business I've seen it all. You'd think I'd be hardened to it by now. But it still bothers the heck out of me."

"Yeah," Brady agreed, his voice thick. "Me, too."

"I feel badly for Lass," Ethan went on. "From what you tell me, and from what I saw at the party, she sounds like a nice young woman."

She was more than nice, Brady thought. She was compassionate, caring, genuine. She deserved a family who loved her. A family like his. But it looked as though Ward Porter was going to arrive tomorrow and change all of that.

"Well, to be fair, we've not heard his side of the story," Brady muttered. "All I can say is that it better be a good one."

Ethan cast him a narrowed glanced. "So when you get to the ranch, what are you going to tell Lass?"

Lifting his Stetson from his head, Brady swiped a shaky hand over his hair. "I don't have much choice. I have to tell her that her father is coming for her," he said flatly. "And I have no idea how she's going to react."

Rising from his chair, Ethan rounded the desk and with a hand on Brady's shoulder, urged him toward the door.

"You've done more than enough for today. Get home and give Lass the news. You can let me know what happens after Mr. Porter arrives tomorrow. And whatever you do,

Brady, don't let him take her without showing you the proper legal documents."

As far as Brady was concerned the man needed to show more than a few paper documents to prove himself worthy of taking Lass anywhere. But he was only a lawman, sworn to protect a person's legal rights, not their future happiness.

"You don't have to worry about that, Ethan. I'm going to make sure Ward Porter is the real thing."

An hour later, he arrived at the ranch and, other than the hired help, discovered the house empty. Even his grandmother was nowhere to be found, which was probably for the best, he thought, as he took the stairs to his bedroom two at a time. He wanted to go straight to Lass with this news. She deserved to hear it before anyone else.

Hurriedly, he changed out of his uniform, then drove over the mountain to Angel Wing Stables. The afternoon was warm and sunny and when he parked his truck in front of the main barn, he noticed that most all the activity appeared to be off to the right in the outdoor arena.

Climbing out of the truck, he headed in that direction only to be intercepted by Dallas, leading a chestnut pony behind her.

"Well, my little brother has finally resurfaced," she said with a grin, then teased, "We were beginning to think we were going to have to drag out the family album to remember what you look like."

"It's been hectic," he explained. "A couple of deputies have been off sick and another with a family emergency. The department's been flooded with calls and working shorthanded made things even worse."

"I'm sorry," Dallas said and as she studied his strained

features, her expression turned to one of concern. "You look so worn, Brady. Is anything wrong?"

He gave her a short nod. "I have news about Lass's case. I need to talk to her about it."

Sensing his urgency but having the tact not to question him, she said, "You should find her in the saddling corral."

"Thanks," he said, then turned to start in that direction.

Before he could take a step, Dallas caught his arm and he arched an inquisitive brow at her.

"What?" he asked.

Smiling, she suggested, "Maybe it would be better if you talked with Lass in private."

"It would. Are you offering me the use of your office?" he asked.

"No. That place isn't private. The staff comes and goes all the time. I was thinking you ought to drive her up to the old foreman's house. I'd been planning on taking a few of the kids up there for a little cookout sometime soon, so I stocked the place with food last week. The two of you could relax without anyone bothering you."

He couldn't have been more grateful to his sister and he quickly leaned forward and pressed a kiss to her cheek. "Thanks, sis. You're my favorite."

"And don't forget it," Dallas called out as he turned and trotted away from her.

The saddling corral was a small lot connected to a row of stalls where many of the Angel Wing horses were kept on a daily basis. When he stepped through a wide, wooden gate, he spotted Lass walking beneath the portico at the far end of the shed row. A saddle pad was bunched beneath her arm while Tyler was trailing after her, his gait stiff from the brace on his leg, but doggedly steady. She'd changed the boy, Brady realized. Just as she'd changed him.

"Hello, you two," Brady called out to them.

Both Lass and Tyler turned at the sound of his voice and as he watched a bright smile light her face, Brady felt something stab him directly in the heart. Was he about to lose this woman forever?

Oh, God, he couldn't think it. Not now.

"Hi, Brady," Tyler greeted. "Have you come to ride with us today?"

"Maybe some other time, partner," Brady told the boy. "Right now, I need to see if I can borrow our girl for a little while. Think you can manage without her?"

Tyler threw his little shoulders back proudly. "Sure, I can manage. Dallas is gonna let me brush Cloudwalker and help saddle him. So I'm gonna be busy anyway." He held up a bridle for Brady to see. "I got to pick out his bridle today. See, it has silver and—" he looked to Lass for help "—what is that other stuff, Lass?"

She smiled. "Copper."

"Yeah. Copper. It has all that fancy stuff on it. It's neat, huh?"

Reaching out, Brady gently scuffed his knuckles against the boy's cheek. "Hoppy couldn't have done better."

Tyler's expression wrinkled with confusion. "Hoppy? Who's that?"

Brady and Lass both laughed, then Brady promised, "Hopalong Cassidy, a famous cowboy. I'll tell you all about him sometime."

At that moment, Dallas hurried up to join them.

"Come on, Ty, let's get that horse of yours saddled before the sun goes down," she said, then gave a subtle signal to Brady and Lass to hit the trail.

As the two of them headed out of the corral, Lass shot him a glowing smile. "Do you know how happy I am to see you?"

At that moment, it was all Brady could do to keep from pulling her into his arms and kissing her. But with children milling about, he couldn't take the chance, because he knew that once his lips touched hers, he wouldn't be able to control his hunger.

"When you left my bed the other night, I had no idea we were going to be apart this long," he explained. "Things have been…worse than hectic. But I'll explain all that later. Right now we're leaving here. I've already talked to Dallas."

She stared at him in surprise. "Leaving? Why?"

He grimaced. "Because—we need to talk."

Picking up the serious note in his voice, she nodded in silent agreement. "I'll go get my things and meet you at your truck."

The old foreman's house was a small stucco structure built on the side of the mountain about a mile from where the riding stables were located. The road up to the old empty home place wasn't graveled, but since the last rain was long ago it had dried up to make the narrow path hard packed and easy to navigate.

As they climbed the twisting road, through a thick stand of juniper, Lass looked at him in confusion. "Why are we going on this road? I thought you said we needed to talk."

"We're going somewhere quiet," he answered. "You'll understand when we get there."

"Why don't we talk now?" she asked, and then slanted him a confused glance. "Are you angry with me about something, Brady?"

Realizing she didn't understand anything that was going on, he reached across the console between their seats, to clasp her hand. "No. I'm not angry at all. Why would I be?"

Her gaze dropped to her lap. "I'm not sure," she said

quietly. "You seem upset. Maybe…you're regretting the other night…when we made love." Her head came up and she squared around in the seat to look at him. "Maybe you're wishing that it never happened, that I…hadn't fallen in love with you."

She looked miserable and Brady felt even worse. Groaning, he shook his head. "No! I'm upset because—" His jaw tightened as they topped a steep rise then flattened out directly in front of the old stucco. "Here we are. Let's go in."

Even though the cool evening air had already started to move in, the house was stuffy from being closed up. While Brady opened the windows, Lass walked around, gazing at the rustic surroundings, but not really seeing anything. She was too anxious and keyed up to concentrate on her surroundings. Whatever it was that Brady had to say, she wanted him to get it over with.

The tenseness she was feeling must have shown on her face because the moment he returned to her side, he gently took hold of her arm and led her over to a small, wood-framed couch. "Let's sit down," he suggested, "so we can be comfortable."

Lass sank next to him on the green cushions and while she waited for him to continue, her thoughts rolled over the past few days since his work schedule had gone awry. Without his company, she'd felt empty and as each day had come and gone, she'd imagined how it would be once he was back home and they finally had a chance to be together. Her whole body had been hungering, pining for him, and she'd envisioned him swooping her up into his arms and kissing her until they were both breathless. Had their time apart caused his desire for her to wane?

"I have news for you," he said finally. "And I wanted us to be alone when I gave it to you."

The grim look on his face put a chill in her heart. "What sort of news?" she asked hoarsely. "Is it…about me? My case?"

He wiped a hand over his face, then swallowed as though his throat was so lodged with words none of them could get out. "I don't know any other way to tell you this, Lass, except that I—"

His troubled gaze caught hers and she inwardly shivered at the dark, foreboding shadows she saw in his green eyes. "I believe I've found your father."

Incredulous, her head reared back as she stared at him. "My…father!" she spluttered. "I thought— Oh, God, I thought you were only going to say that you'd found someone else who'd recognized me being in Ruidoso. This is… Are you sure?"

"Not a hundred percent. But close to it."

Unconsciously her fingertips lifted to her mouth as her breaths started coming fast and short. "Oh, Brady, how—"

"The brand on your old horse, Rusty. It was an *F* that went with the *P*. An *F* for Farms. Porter Farms. Does that ring a bell?"

She closed her eyes as all sort of images began to fly at her like whirling debris in the spin of a tornado. Rooms and furnishings. Barns and stalls. Large trees and thick St. Augustine grass covering the lawn like green carpet. She could almost smell the grill on the patio, the mockingbirds chirping in the live oaks, her mother's sweet voice calling to her, calling out her name.

"Oh, God," she whispered in awe. "My name is Camille! Camille Porter."

A heavy breath rushed out of him and she opened her eyes to see his expression had turned to one of a sad sort of acceptance. His reaction didn't make sense to her. In fact, it scared her and she flung her arms around his neck and held on tightly.

"Brady, what does this all mean? What's going to happen now?"

His arms circled around her and pulled her so close she could scarcely breathe. "Your father is coming tomorrow. I'm figuring he has plans to take you back home with him. Do you remember his name?"

Her face buried in the side of his neck, she continued to cling to him. "No. But I can visualize him now. He— I was very angry with him when I left the ranch. I remember that much. I think I've been angry with him for a long time. Each time I picture him—the two of us together—I feel this huge sense of betrayal and disappointment, but I can't remember why I should feel that way." Lifting her head from his shoulder, she looked at him with sudden conviction. "I don't want to go back with him, Brady. I—"

"Oh, Lass, sweet Lass, don't go getting all worked up right now. We don't know what's going to happen yet."

Another thought struck her, and she untangled herself from his arms and rose to her feet.

"Brady, did he… Did you find out about the man? The one who took me from the racetrack? Did my father mention him or a…husband?"

"No. If this man truly is your father, he didn't mention you having any sort of family. And when I first talked to his secretary she only mentioned Mr. Porter and a daughter. I didn't bring up the subject of the man at the racetrack. To him or the secretary. I didn't want to tip our hand."

She stared at him. "What do you mean?"

Rising from the couch, he closed his hands over her shoulders. "Lass, as a lawman I have to keep my mind open to any and every thing. If Ward Porter had any sort of connection to the man at the racetrack, I want to question him about it before he has a chance to plan his answers."

Stunned, her head jerked back and forth with disbelief. "Do you think… Oh, surely my father didn't send him to harm me?"

The horror of that thought filled her eyes with tears and then she gripped the sides of her head with both hands and moaned. "I can't think, Brady," she said, her voice full of anguish. "Everything is rushing at me. Emotions. Memories. Fears. Oh, God, it has to end! No matter what happens to me, it has to end!"

Her knees suddenly grew so mushy that she was forced to grab the front of his shirt to prevent her body from sliding to the floor.

Muttering a curse, Brady quickly swept her up in his arms and carried her to the back of the house to one of its two bedrooms.

As soon as he deposited her on the bed, she rolled to her side and pressed a hand to her forehead. "I'm sorry, Brady. I just got a little shaky there for a moment."

"Lie still and don't talk," he ordered. "I'll be right back."

By the time he returned with a cool glass of water, she was feeling stronger. After she took several long sips from the glass, he placed it on a nearby dresser, then took a seat on the edge of the mattress.

"Better now?" he asked.

She nodded weakly. "At least my head doesn't feel like it's going to rip apart."

"I should call Bridget to come look you over. Or take you into the hospital," he suggested, his expression tight with concern.

Sighing, she turned on her back and looked up at him. "I

don't need medical attention, Brady. I need time to absorb all of this. It's…too much for me to deal with all at once."

He stroked the hair off her forehead. "I knew this wasn't going to be easy for you. It's not…easy for me, either."

With a look of anguish she rose to a sitting position and cupped his face with her hands. "Brady, I'm so scared. What's going to happen to me?"

Gathering her close to him, he spoke close to her ear. "Nothing is going to happen to you, Lass."

"It will," she sobbed into his shirt. "If I have to leave you."

Suddenly his hands were on her face, tilting her head back and away from him. She blinked away the moisture in her eyes to see that he was gazing at her with hunger and need and something she'd not ever seen on his face before.

"Lass, ever since the night we made love—no even before that—I knew that you were special, I could feel something happening between us. I didn't want to think I was falling in love with you. I thought that was something that would happen a few years down the road, when I was good and ready to let it happen." His mouth twisted to a rueful grin. "I didn't understand it was something a person couldn't control."

Her heart seemed to stop as it waited, wondered, hoped that she was hearing the very thing it needed to survive. "Brady, are you—are you telling me that you love me?"

His fingers delved into her hair, stroked ever so softly against her temple. "I'm telling you that I love you, Lass."

Tears brimmed over the rim of her eyes and slipped down her cheeks. "Are you saying this because you…think it's something I want to hear?"

An anguished groan growled deep in his throat. "Oh, Lass, how could you think that? I…wasn't going to tell you. Not now. Not with everything else that's going on. You already have more than enough to deal with."

"But…don't you understand, Brady? All this other stuff about me—about my past—it doesn't matter. Hearing you say that you love me is all that I need."

With a rueful shake of his head, he pulled her back to him and buried his face in the side of her hair. "But it does matter, Lass. You can't just wipe away the life you'd been leading, as though it didn't exist. You need to go back—to remember—to face the problems you were having and deal with them. Unless you do that I don't think—" He paused as a heavy breath rushed out of him. "I don't think we could ever be truly happy together."

"But Brady—"

"That man, Lass, the one at the track. If you remember him kissing you, then the two of you must have had some sort of relationship. That's why you need to go back to Porter Farms, to give yourself time to remember what he meant to you. Because I…don't want us being together to be a mistake, Lass."

Pulling back from him, she stared at him in stunned wonder. "Brady, I told you that he was kissing me against my will! He was the one who was trying to hurt me! How do you think I could ever have feelings for him?"

Grimacing, he closed his eyes. "Because I don't know what he meant to you in the first place! Lovers have arguments, Lass. They do and say terrible things to each other. In my line of work I see it all the time. Then after a few days, everything is forgiven and forgotten and the two of them are back together."

"Not with me," she said flatly.

His eyes opened, then narrowed skeptically on her face. "All right. Maybe that man wasn't important to you. So how can you be sure there wasn't someone else?

Someone you'd fallen in love with and you just haven't remembered him yet?"

More tears formed in her eyes, then splashed onto her face. "Because I know I wouldn't feel what I do whenever I touch you, Brady. When I search my heart, all I can find is the love I feel for you."

He stared at her for long moments, and then with a stifled groan, he pressed his cheek against hers. "Oh, Lass, I hope you're right. Because I—I'm not sure I can live without you."

She wanted to assure him that he wouldn't have to, but she held the words back. She understood that nothing she could say now would convince him that her life was meant to be with him. The best she could do to convey her love was to show him, to let her lips, her hands and fingers do all the talking.

"Brady."

Whispering his name was all it took for his lips to latch over hers in a kiss so devouring it snatched her breath and pulled a whimper from deep in her throat. Her mouth couldn't begin to keep up with his rough, hungry search, so she simply surrendered to the thrill of being a captive to his kiss.

Mindlessly, her arms slipped around his neck, while one hand glided up the back of his neck and into his thick hair. The hard heat of his body ignited a fire that flashed through her veins, raced down her spine and blanketed her skin with a shiver of goose bumps.

With a guttural growl, he lowered them until they were both lying crosswise on the soft mattress. With their mouths still fused, their arms and legs entwined, he drank deeply from her lips, then nibbled and kissed his way across her cheeks, up her nose and onto her forehead.

By the time he raised his head and gazed down at her, she was weak with desire and nothing else mattered but him and this moment.

"Lass, this isn't going to fix anything," he murmured with anguish. "Tomorrow—"

"Is just that," she swiftly interrupted. "Tomorrow. I don't want to spend this precious time with you talking about what might happen in the next few days. Just love me. Love me now."

She didn't have to implore him a second time. After a moment's hesitation, his mouth crushed down on hers and for a while all thought of tomorrow was forgotten.

Chapter Thirteen

The next day, shortly after lunch, Brady was sitting in the family room with his grandmother when Reggie came to the door and announced that Ward Porter had arrived and she'd seated him in the parlor.

Thanking the maid, he rose from the long couch, then cast a grim glance at Kate. "Well, Grandma, looks like this is it," he said flatly. "Ever since I plucked Lass up out of that ditch, I've been working toward this day. Funny, now that it's here, I feel like hell."

Sensing her grandson's anguish, Kate laid a hand on his arm. "Do you want me to go with you?"

"No. I'd appreciate it if you'd give me a few minutes to go over a few details with this man, then go up and collect Lass from her bedroom," he told her, then with a grateful pat to her hand, he turned and left the room.

As he walked down the long hallway to the parlor, he

was confident that he could trust his grandmother to give Lass the emotional support she needed before facing her father. Since Lass had come to live on the Diamond D, she and Kate had grown close. The fact that his grandmother clearly loved her only proved to Brady that his feelings for Lass weren't foolish or misguided as Conall had tried to make him believe. But once Lass came down those stairs and met her father, how was she going to feel? Was she going to remember everything? Remember that there was a man somewhere back in Texas that she already loved?

Dear God, facing a gun barrel wasn't nearly as terrifying as the thought of losing her.

Once Brady reached the opening of the long parlor, he paused only for a moment before he stepped into the austere room that was relegated for guests such as Ward Porter.

The man was sitting in a green armchair, his elbows resting on his knees, a black cowboy hat dangling from his two hands. He appeared to be a tall, robust sort of man, but at the moment, his graying head was slightly bowed, as though he was in troubled thought. The idea suddenly had Brady wondering how his own father would be feeling if he learned one of his children had gone missing and couldn't even remember his name. Doyle would be devastated. Could be, this man was, too.

Clearing his throat, Brady swiftly crossed the room. Before he reached Ward Porter, the man lifted his head and studied Brady with a curious squint.

"Good afternoon, Mr. Porter. I'm Brady Donovan," he introduced himself. "The deputy you spoke with yesterday."

He extended his hand to Lass's father and with a look of faint surprise the man rose to his feet to shake it.

"I'm not sure I understand any of this," the man said, a frown furrowing his brow. "I've heard of the Diamond

D horses, of course, though I don't think we've ever met. Is this where Camille has been staying since she lost... her memory?"

Brady gestured for the man to return to his seat, then crossed a short space to sit on the edge of a straight-back chair with a cowhide seat.

"That's right, Mr. Porter. This is my family's home. We thought it would be better for her to stay here than in a shelter in Ruidoso."

"Oh. Well, I'm grateful to you for extending her the hospitality," he said, then added, "And by the way, just Ward will do. No need to be formal, is there?"

As far as Brady could see, Lass didn't physically take after her father. His face was broad, his features on the coarse side. The bit of hair that hadn't yet grayed appeared to be a dirty blond color and his eyes were dark brown, the complete opposite of Lass's soft gray. At the moment the man's narrow gaze was wary and full of confusion.

"No. Not at all," Brady agreed.

Ward suddenly reached for something lying on the floor next to his chair and it was then that Brady noticed the leather briefcase.

"I brought all the papers I think you'll need to verify my identity and my relation to Camille. And a few photos, too. Just in case you have any doubts."

Brady had all sorts of doubts, but he couldn't throw them at the man all at once. Besides, a person usually learned more by listening than questioning, he thought.

"I'll look at them in a few minutes," Brady told him. "Right now I'd like to hear about Lass. You told me yesterday you didn't know where she was or had been."

Ward's brown eyes squinted to mere slits. "Lass? You call her by that name?"

"We didn't know her name," Brady reminded him. "And she didn't want to be called Jane."

His eyes suddenly widened and then a faint pallor came over his cheeks. "Oh. I see."

"Do you?" Brady asked. "Because I'm not sure you understand the hell, the anguish, your daughter has endured these past weeks. No one came forward to identify her. No family or friends. I think she was beginning to think that she had no loved ones or family."

A ruddy red suddenly replaced Ward's ghostly white complexion. "Look, maybe I don't come across as father of the year here, but I was in the dark about this whole thing," Ward blurted defensively. "My daughter left the ranch of her own free will. She wouldn't tell me where she was headed. Nothing. And short of following her, there wasn't much I could do to stop her. She's twenty-six years old. That's a grown woman—with her own mind."

The man was clearly agitated, but underneath it all, Brady could see pain on his face, the sort that comes right alongside a dose of regret.

"So you don't know why she came here to New Mexico? To Ruidoso?"

"Not exactly. But I should have guessed. She always loved it out west and she's not going to go anywhere where there's not racehorses close by. That's for damned sure. Guess that's the one thing she got from me." He shoved a hand through his wavy hair, then looked straight at Brady. This time regret and concern were clearly written on the older man's face. "She hasn't remembered me or what happened?"

"Not completely. Only bits and pieces. She claims she was angry with you about something, but she can't remember what or why."

Ward's head suddenly dropped and when he spoke, his

quiet words were directed at the floor. "That much is true," he said with a sigh, then with a rueful twist to his lips, he looked up. "You see, a couple of weeks before Camille left the ranch, her mother passed away. She and Judith had always been really close and her death was almost more than she could bear. Camille is the only child we had and I guess in our own ways we clung to our little girl too much."

Brady leaned forward in his chair as his mind turned over the image of Lass grieving. Just the idea made his heart ache. "Was your wife's death sudden?"

"No. It was an expected thing. She had cancer and her health had quickly deteriorated these past few months. You see, she refused to take any sort of treatments to save her life. And…well, Camille blames me for that. She blames me for her mother's death."

Ward's voice cracked on his last words and Brady wondered how it could get any worse for this man and for Lass.

"Why is that?"

Ward suddenly rose from his chair and with his hands jammed deep in the pockets of his western trousers began to pace around the large room. "Because, damn it, she found out about Jane. My mistress."

"Oh, I see."

He stopped in midstride to look at Brady. "I doubt it," he said tightly. "I doubt your father is…as weak as I am, I'll bet he's always done the right thing, been a man you can look up to."

"Pretty much so. That's not to say he's perfect. He's made some mistakes, but when he does, he'll be the first to admit it."

Tilting his head back, Ward gazed at the high ceiling above their heads. "I could go into a lot of reasons why I've had Jane in my life for the past several years. But that won't fix anything with Camille. She's lost her respect for me. I doubt she'll ever forgive me."

Brady studied him thoughtfully. "I wouldn't say that. She has a huge, compassionate heart. She just needs time. She's been through some trauma and the doctors aren't certain when or if she might recover all her memory."

"Yeah. Well, once I get her back on the farm, I'm going to do everything I can to make it up to her. To help her remember."

Drawing in a deep, bracing breath, Brady rose to his feet. "Ward, I've not asked this yet, but before she left the ranch was Lass involved with anyone?"

Brady's question caused the older man's brows to arch with faint surprise. "Involved? You mean with a man?"

The urge to swallow at the hard lump in his throat was so great Brady finally had to cough before he could speak. "That's what I mean. Like a husband? Fiancé? Boyfriend?"

"No. Camille has only had a handful of boyfriends over the past years and none of them have been that serious. Her mother always said our daughter put her love into horses, not men. That's why she's not yet gotten married. I say she's just darned picky. I've tried my best to get her interested in David, one of my assistant trainers, but she wouldn't have any part of him." His gaze narrowed on Brady's face. "Why do you ask?"

Now was hardly the time for Brady to go into his feelings for Lass. There were still many blank spaces that needed to be filled in. If not by this man, then someone he might lead to.

"Your daughter was injured because she was running from a man. A man who was seen with her at the track. She remembers struggling with him, but she can't yet identify him. I thought you might have an idea of who this person could have been."

Ward looked disgusted and horrified at the same time and Brady instinctively knew that he'd played no part in Lass's injury.

"I don't have a clue. None of her friends back home would do such a vile thing. And she's...well, she's always been a good girl. She wouldn't have let herself be picked up by a strange man at the track. It would have been done against her will."

Yes, she was a good girl, a good person, Brady silently agreed. She deserved to be happy and now that he'd talked with Ward, he could see that she needed to return to Porter Farms, needed to get her feet under her and her past in order before she could truly be ready to start a life, a family with him. If that meant he had to hand her over to this man, for however long it took, then he would. Because he loved her. Because in spite of everything, what he wanted the most was her happiness.

Dear God, was this the first time in his life that he'd put a woman's feelings before his own desires? The idea stung him, made him wonder what he'd been doing, thinking?

Hell, you know what you've been doing, Brady. You've always thought love was just a game you could either play or leave on the table. Now Lass has come along and showed you that love is nothing about playing or lust or getting what you desire. It's about caring, protecting, giving.

Shaken by the idea that these past few weeks with Lass had changed him so much, he turned away from her father and swallowed hard. "That's my thought, too."

The sound of footsteps suddenly caught both men's attention and Brady turned to see Lass and his grandmother stepping into the room. Kate had her arm around Lass's shoulders, yet even with the older woman's support, Brady could see she was walking gingerly, as though meeting her father had left her weak and wary.

He could hear the slight intake of Ward's breath before he took one step toward his daughter, then stopped abruptly and stared at her.

Across the room Lass could feel Kate's strong arm at her waist, supporting her, comforting her, yet in spite of the woman's hold on her, she felt as though her legs were going to crumble.

The man standing in front of her was her father. All this time, how could she not have remembered his name, his face? Now that she was seeing him in the flesh, it seemed incredible that her mind could have erased so much.

"Camille. Honey."

From the corner of her eyes, Lass could see Brady moving to join them and her heart ached as she thought about the sweet love they'd made last night in the foreman's old house. Was he actually going to force her to leave the Diamond D? Leave him? She couldn't think about it now. If she did, she would totally break apart.

Once she was finally standing face-to-face with her father, Brady and Kate discreetly moved aside. Lass felt lost without them and the notion only proved how much at home she felt on the Diamond D, how much she considered Brady's family as her family. Even Doyle, who wasn't around all that much of the time, seemed more like a father to her now than Ward Porter.

"Hello, Daddy," she quietly greeted.

For a moment he said nothing and then his face crumpled and his voice was full of cracks when he finally spoke. "You…remember me?"

Lass nodded. "Much more clearly now."

Behind her right shoulder, Kate cleared her throat. "If you'll all excuse me, I'll get Opal to prepare a tray of refreshments."

"I'll carry it back for you," Brady said, then turned to follow his grandmother out of the room.

Panicked by the thought of being without him, Lass blurted, "No, Brady! Please, come here. With me."

He came to stand beside her and a small breath of relief rushed out of her as his arm settled at her waist. This was the man she loved, the man she always wanted at her side. Without him only half of her would exist.

"Honey," Ward began, "you didn't leave any word about where you were going. You wouldn't answer your phone. I thought you were still hiding out somewhere just to spite me. I had no idea that you were lost. That you'd had some sort of accident. If I had, I would have been here immediately."

Lass glanced up at Brady's strong profile. "Maybe it's best you hadn't known where to find me," she said softly.

Ward's narrowed gaze traveled back and forth between his daughter and the deputy who'd rescued her. "How are you feeling now?" he asked Lass. "Ready to make the trip back to Porter Farms?"

"I don't think I want to go to Porter Farms with you," she said flatly.

Brady shot her a stunned look while Ward impatiently shook his head.

"Let's not start this again, Camille."

"I'm not Camille anymore. I prefer the name Lass now," she bluntly pointed out.

Gasping with outrage, the older man looked to Brady. "What have you people done to her? What have *you* done to her? Brainwashed her? Can't you see that she's confused? She's not even sure of her own name!"

Something about the sound of her father's angry voice pierced her and suddenly layers and layers of images were rapidly unfolding in her mind. They were coming at her with such a rush that she was close to being ill, yet at the same time relief was flooding through her, replacing all her doubts and uncertainties with a furious sort of confidence.

"No one has tried to brainwash me, Daddy. Except maybe you. Brainwash me into thinking that your and Jane's trysts were something acceptable, that your long-term affair had nothing to do with Mother's death. Well, you can tell yourself that if it makes you feel better, but you'll never convince me! Mother let herself die because she didn't want to live with a cheating husband. You were her whole life and you betrayed her with an old family friend. You betrayed me."

"Camille! This is not the time or place to be sorting our family laundry! Now get your things. We're leaving. Before we say something that can never be taken back."

Completely ignoring Ward, Lass whipped around to Brady. Excitement, amazement and joy all swept across her face as she gazed up at him. "There's no need for me to go back to Porter Farms now, Brady! I remember everything. And I can tell you now that I'm free. Free to stay here and love you."

A tender light filled his eyes and then before Ward could say anything about the matter, Brady swept her into his arms and kissed her. As the tender touch of his lips lingered on hers, Lass felt contentment so sweet and pure that tears flooded her eyes.

"What is going on here?" Ward demanded.

Just as Brady lifted his head to explain, the doorbell rang. Since Reggie was nowhere to be seen, Brady set Lass aside to go answer it.

"Excuse me," he said as he quickly strode toward the foyer. "I'll be right back."

Once Brady was out of sight, Ward stepped closer to his daughter. "Do you love that young man? Is that why you don't want to come home with me?"

Lass's lips trembled. Her father had hurt her, had managed to destroy her admiration for him, scar all the good years when her family had been happy, when her family's love was whole and strong. And yet, a part of her still loved him, didn't want to lose her only parent.

"I do love him, Daddy. But I—" She swallowed hard, then dismally shook her head. "My life at Porter Farms is over. I think we both realized that once Mother died and I…found out about Jane." A rueful grimace twisted her features. "I'm not saying I want to shut you out of my life completely. I'm trying to tell you that I need time. Time to try to make sense of all that's happened to our family."

He reached out and gingerly touched her cheek. "All I ask is for a chance to make it up to you, honey," he said brokenly. "You and your mother—you've always been my whole life. All I've ever worked for—the farm, the horses—it was for you."

Her throat burning, she turned her face away from him and blinked her eyes. "Yes, I know," she murmured thickly.

The sound of footsteps came from across the room and both Lass and Ward turned to see Brady emerge from the foyer. Another man was following directly behind him, but his head was hidden by Brady's broad shoulder.

Since the Donovans didn't carry out ranching business in the house, Lass wondered if the unannounced guest was Sheriff Hamilton, wanting to question her father. But then Brady suddenly stepped to one side and she could see the visitor was not the rugged sheriff; it was her nightmare come to life.

"David," Ward greeted warmly, "did you have a good look at the Donovans' stables?"

Lass stared numbly at the man, her throat too paralyzed to utter a sound.

He glanced over at Lass, then gave her a sympathetic smile as though she didn't have her full mental faculties and needed to be treated with patience and understanding. Clearly he'd made this trip with Ward confident that Lass still had amnesia and wouldn't be able to recognize him, she thought wildly.

Turning his attention to her father, he answered, "It was great, Ward. You really need to let Mr. Donovan show you around before we leave. They have an aquatic pool for the horses and I want you to see it. I think it's time Porter Farms invested in one. If we plan to compete—"

The muscles in Lass's throat finally released enough to work and she screamed loudly as she stumbled backward, away from David and her father.

Brady leaped forward and caught her by the arm. "Lass! What is it? What's wrong?"

Horrified, she flung a finger toward David, who was already backing cautiously away from them. "David—he's the one who attacked me! At the car—in the mountains!"

Feigning a wounded expression, David stepped forward and held his palms upward in a gesture of innocence. "Camille, I'm so sorry about your—accident. Your father tells me you can't remember anything and I can see for myself how tangled your thinking is right now. But you'll get well and then you'll see how much I care about you."

He reached a hand toward her and Lass shrank back against the comfort of Brady's solid frame.

"Liar!" she flung at him. "You—you're psychotic. Tell my father what you were planning to do to me! To him!"

Totally confused, Ward turned to his daughter and said in a soothing, placating voice. "Honey, you're confused. That's David. Our assistant. Our friend. Remember? He couldn't be the man who tried to harm you."

"He's not a friend, Daddy," she spoke through gritted teeth. "All he wanted was to get your ranch and he planned to do that through me. I tried to tell you about him months ago, but you refused to believe me! Now after all that's happened, you're still taking his side!"

Apparently Ward's spoken defense of him was enough to give David the courage to stop his backward progression out of the room and he stared at Lass as though he couldn't believe she would have the gall or the courage to accuse him of anything.

He said, "Camille, you're still a sick woman. You obviously have me confused with some other man."

Her voice trembling, Lass shouted at him, "I'm sick all right for not screaming to high heaven at the track when you strong-armed me into your car!"

Ward's bewildered expression suddenly turned suspicious as he looked at his assistant. "A few days after Camille left the ranch, you made a trip to Florida to visit your family. Or so you said. Maybe Deputy Donovan should give them a call and straighten out this matter," Ward suggested.

David's gaze was suddenly darting nervously around the room. "This from you, Ward? I'm going outside for some fresh air and while I'm gone maybe you'll come to your senses and realize your daughter is delusional."

"Come here!" The order to David came from Brady, his

voice steely soft and so menacing it could have been a weapon. "You have a few questions to answer."

"Not to you, buddy!"

At that moment David turned and started to run toward the foyer, but Brady instantly leaped into action and halfway across the room, he caught Lass's attacker by the arm and spun him around.

David immediately resisted and attempted to throw a punch at Brady's face, but he quickly dodged the blow. David attempted to swing again, but by then Brady was plowing into him with both fists, until he staggered backward then fell against an antique table. The piece of furniture, along with an ornate lamp, crashed to the floor. David followed close behind and lay sprawled and groaning among the broken pieces.

"My God!" Ward bellowed in stunned disbelief. "What is going on here?"

Heaving from anger and exertion, Brady glanced at him. "You're witnessing an arrest. Lincoln County style."

"Then I'm here at the perfect time," Kate announced as she hurried into the room. She was carrying a large silver tray and there, among the drinks and snacks, lay a pair of handcuffs. With a catlike grin, she shoved the tray toward Brady. "I heard the commotion and thought you might need these."

Wiping his sweaty forehead against the sleeve of his shirt, Brady looked at her and the handcuffs, then started to chuckle. "Grandma, are these the cuffs I gave you as a gag gift?"

Kate chuckled along with her grandson. "I knew someday I'd have good use for them."

Grabbing up the cuffs, he planted a kiss on her cheek. "I can never get ahead of you, can I?"

She tossed him a grin full of love and pride. "Don't even try."

Quickly, Brady plucked the woozy man from the floor and cuffed his hands behind his back. Once he was certain his prisoner was securely shackled, he shoved him down in the nearest chair and turned to search the room for Lass.

She was standing only a few feet away, anxiously waiting and watching for the ordeal to be over. As soon as he held out his arms, she ran to him and buried her face against his chest.

"Oh, Brady," she sobbed with relief. "My nightmare is finally over."

Pressing his cheek to the top of her head, he held her tightly. "And our life together is just beginning, my darling."

Later that night, in the privacy of the foreman's old house, Lass and Brady lay snuggled together on the small double bed. An arm's width away, moonlight slanted through the bare windows and bathed Lass's face in a silver glow that matched the radiant light in her eyes.

Even though she was drowsy from their lovemaking, she couldn't seem to wipe the smile from her face or to let herself actually fall asleep. There was too much to think about, too much to experience to waste it on slumber.

Drawing lazy circles across Brady's chest, she tilted her head back far enough to see his face. His tawny hair lay in rumpled waves over his forehead while his relaxed features were a total contrast to the fierce expression he'd had when he'd lunged for David.

"Are you sorry that Grandma invited Ward to stay on the ranch with us for a few days?" Brady asked in a dozy voice. "She really wasn't trying to butt in, you know. She loves you."

The corners of Lass's lips continued to curve upward. "Yes, I know she loves me. And she wants me and my father to have a chance to talk things over and hopefully make a new start of things. She believes that's important to my happiness."

"So do I." His fingers gently stroked her hair. "Do you think it's possible for the two of you to start over?"

"I didn't before. But I do now. I think…when the awful truth about David finally sunk in, I believe he realized how he'd been looking at things in the wrong way. You see, my father has always been a hard-driving, ambitious man. And David is that same type. I suppose that's why he liked him so much. Why he wouldn't believe me when I told him that he was making overtures that were making me… uncomfortable."

"Had David worked for your family long?"

"Probably three years. And in that time I made the mistake of going out on one date with him. It took me about an hour to realize he wasn't my type at all. But he refused to accept that I had no interest in him." She sighed. "What will happen to him now, Brady?"

Earlier this afternoon, after things had calmed down, Brady had hauled David to the jail in Carrizozo. As of now, the man was still behind bars, waiting for bail to be set.

"That's for a court to decide, Lass. As far as I'm concerned they should lock him away for a long while. But I can't believe that all this while he was checking in to make sure you still had amnesia and couldn't identify him. It took a lot of nerve to come face you again. He sounds like the kind of man who thinks if he wants it hard enough it will come true."

Lass shivered. Now that her memory had returned, the images of what had happened continued to haunt her. Yet a part of her was glad that she could remember the whole incident now. Remember it and hopefully come to terms with it all.

"When he showed up at the track, I was stunned, Brady. I was standing there at the saddling paddock watching the jockeys and the horses and then suddenly David showed up out of nowhere. I had no idea that he knew I'd come here to New Mexico. The only thing I can figure is that he overheard my phone conversation when I was making flight plans."

"What did he tell you? I mean, the reason that he was there?"

"He'd said that my father had taken ill and that he'd come to fetch me home."

"The man hadn't heard of telephoning?" Brady asked.

"Exactly," she answered. "I was immediately suspicious, so I told him I wanted to call my father first. That's when he jerked the cell phone from my hand and forcefully walked me to his car."

Brady made a tsking noise with his tongue. "Bad mistake, Lass. Never get into a car with someone you don't trust."

"I certainly learned that lesson," she said wryly. "I made a huge mistake by not making a scene at the track and alerting someone that I needed help. I should have never allowed him to get me into the car. But I went along. Because deep down, I never suspected he would try to physically harm me. But then as we drove east from the track, he begin to tell me how much he loved me, how once Daddy was dead, the two of us could have Porter Farms for our own. I was terrified. He seemed so calm, so sure that once he'd had me on his own I'd be willing to stay with him and let him have control of me and the ranch. He talked about giving me tranquilizers and telling everyone I'd had a breakdown after my mother died, but he was going to care for me. Or that I'd even have an accident if I ever tried to leave him."

Brady propped himself up on one shoulder to look down

at her. "God, Lass, do you think he meant to murder your father? Or did he only mean when your father grew older and passed away?"

Lass shook her head. "I'm not certain. But when he said those things, there was evilness in his voice that I'd never heard before. After that my mind began to work furiously to find a way to get out of the car and away from him. I knew if I ever had a chance of escape I would have to do it while we were still in the mountains. Once we got out on the flat desert there wouldn't be anywhere to hide. So I feigned nausea and told him to pull the car over before I retched everywhere."

"Yes. Johnny found the spot where the car was parked," Brady said. "He said a scuffle happened there."

Lass closed her eyes against the vivid memories. "David got out of the car, too. I guess by then, he didn't trust me. I walked to the trunk area and began to cough, but it wasn't convincing enough for him. He grabbed me with intentions of putting me back in the car. He told me it was time he had a bit of fun."

"Bastard," Brady cursed. "I should have hit him again, just for good measure."

She slipped a hand down his muscled arm. He was a strong man, this man that she loved and he would always be there to fight for her, protect her in every way. It was a heady thought.

"That's exactly what I did," she told him. "Hard. I guess he wasn't expecting me to fight back. Especially me jabbing my fingers in his eyes. While he was howling, I ran. The sun had gone down, but there was still a bit of light left. He chased after me, but I suppose he couldn't see very well because of what I'd done to his eyes. Once I climbed out of the ravine, I lost him and kept running up the mountain. Until I fell. Then the next thing I remember is waking up to see your face hovering over me."

A tender smile curved his lips. "And now you're here. Still in my arms. I just can't get rid of you, can I?"

"Do you want to?" she asked in a voice that was half-teasing, half-serious.

Brady's eyes twinkled. "I'm not sure. Maybe you'd better let me think about this before I answer."

"I probably should. Since you know very little about my past."

"What's there to know that I need to know?"

"Hmm. Well, let's see, I made straight A's in high school and I took choir all four years."

One of his brows arched upward. "You can sing?"

"Only in the shower."

He grinned. "Good. That means you can serenade me."

She laughed softly. "And I graduated from TU with a degree in business. I used that knowledge to help with the business side of Porter Farms. But horses are my first love. Working with them is what I've always wanted to do the most. Does that bother you?"

"Only if you spend more time with them than me."

She trailed the tip of her index finger across his chin. "I promise to never let that happen."

"Does it bother you that I'm a lawman?"

Suddenly serious, she said, "It worries me that your job sometimes puts you in danger. But I've seen a jockey break his neck. Everything has its dangers. That's why we need to live and love and enjoy each other as much as we can, whenever we can."

"You got that right," he murmured, then tilting his head, he kissed her softly, slowly, as he tried to convey with his lips all the love he was feeling in his heart.

Once he lifted his head, he announced, "We're going to be married. As soon as we can make the arrangements."

Her hands came up to cup gently frame his face. "Are you sure that's what you want, Brady? There's no urgency for us to become man and wife right now. And you've been a bachelor for a long time. Maybe you need to wait and think about this," she suggested.

His brows pulled together. "Lass, I'm asking you to marry me! And here you are trying to talk me out of it?"

"I only want you to be happy. And before I came along you were a free man. You liked to date. Different women."

His frown deepened. "Before you came along, I didn't understand anything about needing, loving. I thought playing the field would be all I'd want for a long, long time. I didn't know what it meant to have someone become a part of me. I didn't know that just the thought of having that part of me torn away would be too much to bear."

"You wanted me to go back to Porter Farms. Apparently you believed you could get along without me."

He groaned. "That's because I wanted you to be happy. And I thought it could never happen until you reacquainted yourself with your old life. I never dreamed that everything was suddenly going to come back to you. But I thank God that it did."

He lowered his head, until his lips were poised over hers. "So what is your answer to my proposal? Am I going to have to beg to get a yes out of you?"

"No," she said with a happy sigh. "All you have to do is love me."

"For the rest of my life, darling."

Epilogue

Three months later, on a cold December morning, Lass and Brady stood in the middle of the ranch yard and waved to Dallas as she pulled away in a truck with a horse van attached to the back.

As Lass watched her sister-in-law's vehicle turn a curve and disappear from sight, she said thoughtfully, "Dallas never quits looking for the perfect horse to use at Angel Wing. When Maura mentioned to her that Jake Rollins had an extremely gentle horse for sale, she couldn't wait to drive over to his place to see it."

Brady's mouth took on a rueful slant. "Well, just between you and me, I'd prefer she not do business with Jake."

Lass looked at him with a bit of surprise. Jake was his sister Maura and brother-in-law Quint's ranch foreman. What could Brady have against the man? she wondered.

"Why? He wouldn't do any underhanded horsetrading with Dallas, would he?" she asked.

Brady shook his head. "Not at all. Jake's an honest man. And he's damned good with horses. But he's hell with the ladies. His motto should be too many women and not enough time."

Lass chuckled knowingly. "Seems like I once knew another man around here that was described as a ladies' man."

Wrapping his arm around the back of her waist, he snuggled her close to his side. "Yeah. But that was before I found the love of my life."

She smiled dreamily up at him. "That's probably all that Jake needs to cure his roaming ways—to find the love of his life."

Bending his head, he pressed a kiss on her forehead. "You could be right. After all, you certainly cured me."

Lass said, "Well, if I'd known you were so concerned about Dallas's virtue, I could have made a trip with her to Jake's place this morning. Just to act as chaperone."

Brady laughed. "Oh, no! I'm not that worried about my big sister." With his arm curved possessively around her shoulders, he urged her in the direction of the house. "We both have the day off today and I'm going to take you shopping."

"Shopping!" She shot him a wry look. "You don't care anything about shopping!"

"I do when I go with a purpose. And Christmas is coming. We have all sorts of gifts to buy."

As they continued on toward the house, a dreamy expression drifted over her face. It would be her first Christmas as Brady's wife and this morning she'd learned she was going to be giving him a special gift. Now she was waiting for the right moment to tell him.

"Oh, well, I'd better get my thinking cap on," she told him. "Because I don't have a clue as what to buy you."

He chuckled. "Forget about getting me a gift. I'm a man who has everything."

Lass only smiled.

At the house, they warmed themselves with short cups of coffee, then climbed the stairs to the bedroom they shared. While Brady showered, Lass changed into a long black peasant skirt and topped it with a bright red sweater.

After she'd brushed her hair loose on her shoulders and attached sparkling earrings to her ears, she walked over to the plate glass door leading out to the balcony. This morning the sky was overcast with high gray clouds. Every now and then tiny bits of snow flew through the air.

Already the mountains surrounding the ranch were capped with white and Ruidoso was full of skiers come to enjoy the fresh powder on Sierra Blanca. For Lass, becoming accustomed to the high mountain climate had taken some getting used to. Already the area had been doused with several inches of snow, but she'd learned to dress for the cold and enjoy the winter season. Just as she was learning to be a Donovan and take pleasure in being part of a big family.

Thankfully, even distant Conall had accepted and welcomed her in his own stern way. She felt truly at home now, yet there were moments like this morning, when she'd used the pregnancy test, that she ached to have her mother back with her. There were so many things she wished she could tell her. Like how happy Brady had made her, how much she loved him and how much he loved her. She longed to tell her about her work at the stables, about all the horses she'd grown so attached to, the lovely children who looked to her for help and guidance. And she also wanted Judith to know that her marriage to Ward had not been a complete failure.

These past few months, Lass had tried to open her heart and her mind to her father. They'd had several lengthy talks over the phone and she was beginning to realize that, in spite of his mistakes, Ward had loved his family. After David had pled guilty to his crimes and was sentenced with jail time, her father had taken a new turn with his life. He'd seemed to suddenly realize that he needed to change, to take time for the things that are most important. He'd completely cut ties with Jane and hired a new assistant to fill David's vacancy. He was even coming out to the Diamond D for a visit during the Christmas holiday and this time Lass was actually looking forward to seeing him.

Forgiveness was not an easy thing, she thought, but it was the right thing. She could see that now. And how could she not forgive, when she'd been blessed with so much happiness?

Behind her, she heard the door to the walk-in closet open, then close. Glancing over her shoulder, she saw Brady shrugging into a dark green shirt that made his tawny hair look even more like a wild lion's mane.

Her eyes full of pleasure, she watched him button the shirt as he walked toward her.

"My, my, you're looking too pretty this morning to be going out with a guy like me. Maybe I'd better go back to the closet and pick out something a little fancier than this ol' shirt."

Turning, she reached to fasten the button in the middle of his chest. "I don't want you to change anything. You happen to look very handsome in this shirt."

Smiling, he bent his head and placed a soft kiss on her lips. "Spoken like a true, loving wife."

"I am a true, loving wife."

"You don't have to convince me of that. But you do need to tell me what you'd like for Christmas. I want to give you something really special. Something you'll love for a long time."

Love swelled in her chest. It didn't matter what sort of gifts Brady gave her. The love he put behind them was the thing that made them precious to her.

"Now what are you planning to give me? You don't have to tell me outright. Give me a little hint and let me guess first."

Dimples carved her cheeks as she gazed up at him. "Well, it's already ordered. But I can't tell you precisely what the gift will be until it gets here."

"Hmm. That sounds intriguing."

"More like shocking," she replied as she struggled to keep an ecstatic smile from breaking across her face.

He arched a skeptical brow at her. "Okay, now you've done it. Why can't you tell me—precisely? Because you want it to be a surprise?"

Chuckles bubbled in her throat. "No. Because I wasn't able to make an exact order. I had to leave it up to God to make the final decision. And that's a fifty-fifty tossup. I can only tell you that it will either be a little deputy or a little cowgirl."

Confusion puckered his features and then suddenly it all fell in place. Stunned elation swept over his face as he grabbed her by the shoulders.

"A baby?" he asked incredulously. "You're telling me that we have a baby coming?"

Once Lass nodded, he threw back his head and howled with glee.

"Oh, darling! You've made me the happiest man alive!" Bending his head, he kissed her, then kissed her again. "How will I ever be able to top this Christmas gift you've given me?"

Her eyes misty, she smiled at him. "Oh, I don't know, try for another one next Christmas, I suppose."

Laughing, he ran out of the room and onto the landing. "Hey everybody, come here and listen to this!" he shouted at the top of his lungs. "We're going to have a baby!"

Her heart overflowing with love, Lass left the room to help her husband spread the news.

* * * * *

Will Jake Rollins find the love of his life?
Don't miss the upcoming
MEN OF THE WEST *story from*
Stella Bagwell
Coming in late 2010!

*Harlequin Intrigue top author Delores Fossen
presents a brand-new series of breathtaking
romantic suspense!*
TEXAS MATERNITY: HOSTAGES
*The first installment available May 2010:
THE BABY'S GUARDIAN*

Shaw cursed and hooked his arm around Sabrina.

Despite the urgency that the deadly gunfire created, he tried to be careful with her, and he took the brunt of the fall when he pulled her to the ground. His shoulder hit hard, but he held on tight to his gun so that it wouldn't be jarred from his hand.

Shaw didn't stop there. He crawled over Sabrina, sheltering her pregnant belly with his body, and he came up ready to return fire.

This was obviously a situation he'd wanted to avoid at all cost. He didn't want his baby in the middle of a fight with these armed fugitives, but when they fired that shot, they'd left him no choice. Now, the trick was to get Sabrina safely out of there.

"Get down," someone on the SWAT team yelled from the roof of the adjacent building.

Shaw did. He dropped lower, covering Sabrina as best he could.

There was another shot, but this one came from a rifleman on the SWAT team. Shaw didn't look up, but he heard the sound of glass being blown apart.

The shots continued, all coming from his men, which

meant it might be time to try to get Sabrina to better cover. Shaw glanced at the front of the building.

So that Sabrina's pregnant belly wouldn't be smashed against the ground, Shaw eased off her and moved her to a sitting position so that her back was against the brick wall. They were close. Too close. And face-to-face.

He found himself staring right into those sea-green eyes.

How will Shaw get Sabrina out?
Follow the daring rescue and the heartbreaking
aftermath in THE BABY'S GUARDIAN
by Delores Fossen,
available May 2010 from Harlequin Intrigue.

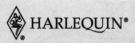
HARLEQUIN®

American ★ Romance®

LAURA MARIE ALTOM

The Baby Twins

Stephanie Olmstead has her hands full raising
her twin baby girls on her own. When she runs
into old friend Brady Flynn, she's shocked to find
herself suddenly attracted to the handsome airline
pilot! Will this flyboy be the perfect daddy—
or will he crash and burn?

Babies
&
Bachelors
USA

"LOVE, HOME & HAPPINESS"

www.eHarlequin.com

HAR75309

HARLEQUIN Ambassadors

Want to share your passion for reading Harlequin® Books?

Become a Harlequin Ambassador!

Harlequin Ambassadors are a group of passionate and well-connected readers who are willing to share their joy of reading Harlequin® books with family and friends.

You'll be sent all the tools you need to spark great conversation, including free books!

All we ask is that you share the romance with your friends and family!

You'll also be invited to have a say in new book ideas and exchange opinions with women just like you!

To see if you qualify* to be a Harlequin Ambassador, please visit www.HarlequinAmbassadors.com.

*Please note that not everyone who applies to be a Harlequin Ambassador will qualify. For more information please visit www.HarlequinAmbassadors.com.

Thank you for your participation.

BAP09BPA

Bestselling Harlequin Presents® author

Lynne Graham

introduces

VIRGIN ON HER WEDDING NIGHT

Valente Lorenzatto never forgave Caroline Hales's
abandonment of him at the altar. But now he's
made millions and claimed his aristocratic Venetian
birthright—and he's poised to get his revenge.
He'll ruin Caroline's family by buying out their
company and throwing them out of their mansion…
unless she agrees to give him the wedding night
she denied him five years ago.…

**Available May 2010
from Harlequin Presents!**

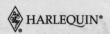

HARLEQUIN® *Blaze*™

is proud to introduce...

New York Times bestselling author

Brenda Jackson

with
SPONTANEOUS

Kim Cannon and Duan Jeffries have a great thing going.
Whenever they meet up, the passion between them
is hot, intense…spontaneous. And things really heat
up when Duan agrees to accompany her to her
mother's wedding. Too bad there's something
he's not telling her….

Don't miss the fireworks!

*Available in May 2010
wherever Harlequin Blaze books are sold.*

---

red-hot reads

REQUEST YOUR FREE BOOKS!

2 FREE NOVELS PLUS 2 FREE GIFTS!

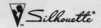

SPECIAL EDITION
Life, Love and Family!

YES! Please send me 2 FREE Silhouette® Special Edition® novels and my 2 FREE gifts (gifts are worth about $10). After receiving them, if I don't wish to receive any more books, I can return the shipping statement marked "cancel." If I don't cancel, I will receive 6 brand-new novels every month and be billed just $4.24 per book in the U.S. or $4.99 per book in Canada. That's a saving of 15% off the cover price! It's quite a bargain! Shipping and handling is just 50¢ per book.* I understand that accepting the 2 free books and gifts places me under no obligation to buy anything. I can always return a shipment and cancel at any time. Even if I never buy another book from Silhouette, the two free books and gifts are mine to keep forever.

235/335 SDN E5RG

Name	(PLEASE PRINT)	

Address		Apt. #

City	State/Prov.	Zip/Postal Code

Signature (if under 18, a parent or guardian must sign)

Mail to the **Silhouette Reader Service:**
IN U.S.A.: P.O. Box 1867, Buffalo, NY 14240-1867
IN CANADA: P.O. Box 609, Fort Erie, Ontario L2A 5X3

Not valid for current subscribers to Silhouette Special Edition books.

Want to try two free books from another line?
Call 1-800-873-8635 or visit www.morefreebooks.com.

* Terms and prices subject to change without notice. Prices do not include applicable taxes. N.Y. residents add applicable sales tax. Canadian residents will be charged applicable provincial taxes and GST. Offer not valid in Quebec. This offer is limited to one order per household. All orders subject to approval. Credit or debit balances in a customer's account(s) may be offset by any other outstanding balance owed by or to the customer. Please allow 4 to 6 weeks for delivery. Offer available while quantities last.

Your Privacy: Silhouette is committed to protecting your privacy. Our Privacy Policy is available online at www.eHarlequin.com or upon request from the Reader Service. From time to time we make our lists of customers available to reputable third parties who may have a product or service of interest to you. If you would prefer we not share your name and address, please check here. ☐

Help us get it right—We strive for accurate, respectful and relevant communications. To clarify or modify your communication preferences, visit us at www.ReaderService.com/consumerschoice.

SSE10R